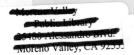

D0977584

Dark
SECRETS

ANNE SCHRAFF

SADDLEBACK
EDUCATIONAL PUBLISHING

URBAN UNDERGROUND

A Boy Called Twister

Dark Secrets

Deliverance

The Fairest

If You Really Loved Me

Leap of Faith

Like a Broken Doll

The Lost

No Fear

One of Us

Outrunning the Darkness

The Quality of Mercy

Shadows of Guilt

The Stranger

Time of Courage

To Be a Man

To Catch a Dream

The Unforgiven

The Water's Edge

Wildflower

SADDLEBACK
EDUCATIONAL PUBLISHING
www.sdlback.com

ISBN-13: 978-1-61651-267-5
ISBN-10: 1-61651-267-9
eBook: 978-1-60291-992-1

Printed in Guangzhou, China
0212/CA21200288

16 15 14 13 12   2 3 4 5

CHAPTER ONE

Calico, the Sandovals' cat, let out a long screech, as Ernesto Sandoval and his family were finishing breakfast. Sixteen-year-old Ernesto was about to take off for Cesar Chavez High School, where he was a junior. His father, Luis Sandoval, was about to head out for the same school, where he taught American and world history.

Juanita, Ernesto's six-year-old sister, ran to the window and screamed, "A big old white dog is chasing Calico. I think he's gonna eat her!"

Maria Sandoval, Ernesto's mother, jumped up, almost knocking over the coffee pot. "Oh my goodness!" she cried.

"We gotta save poor Calico," eight-year-old Katalina shouted.

Ernesto was immediately at the back door, his father right behind him. "It's Brutus, that pit bull the Martinez family got," Ernesto shouted. He rushed into the yard to get between the dog and Calico. But Calico had already escaped up the pepper tree. She now sat crouched, trembling, on a limb. "It's okay, Mom," Ernesto hollered. "Calico is safe."

Both Ernesto and his father were tall and skinny, but they were tough. They approached the pit bull, which was barking and leaping at the trunk of the pepper tree.

"Brutus!" Ernesto yelled in as commanding a voice as he could muster. Ernesto didn't care much for the dog's owner, Felix Martinez. But he deeply cared about Naomi, Mr. Martinez's daughter and a beautiful junior at school. Felix Martinez had bought the pit bull against his wife's wishes. Now Linda Martinez was so terrified of the dog that she was always afraid in her own house. Ernesto thought that buying the dog had been a mean thing for Felix Martinez to do. The man seemed to have a sadistic streak. He enjoyed seeing other people afraid because then he could look down on them. He could feel better than them because he wasn't afraid of anything.

Mom came outside and handed Ernesto a length of rope. Ernesto and his father then cornered Brutus by the tool shed. Ernesto spoke softly to the dog. "Come on, boy. Settle down. We want to take you home. You wanna go home, right? Sure you do." As he spoke, Ernesto gently slipped the rope through the ring on the dog's collar and tied it.

"Ernie, be careful," Mom cautioned.

Luis Sandoval was right beside Ernesto, helping him calm the pit bull down. "I don't think he's vicious," Dad remarked. "But you never know. You hear so many bad things about this breed . . . "

Ernesto smiled as he stood up, holding onto the rope. "That wasn't bad, eh Brutus?

You're just a big old puppy, eh Brutus? You don't want to bite anybody."

"That was good, Ernie," Dad commented. "You handled that real well."

"Dad, you should see how scared Mrs. Martinez is of this dog," Ernesto said. "Her husband told me he got the dog just to force her to overcome her fears. But half the time she locks herself in the kitchen so Brutus can't get at her. I don't know, Dad. I think there's something wrong with a guy who does that to his wife."

Dad said nothing. But he had a hard look on his face, as if he knew about the situation at the Martinez house. He seemed to be aware of some dark secrets in that place. "They live over on Bluebird, right?" Dad asked.

"Yeah," Ernesto replied. "I can take Brutus home before I go to school. It'll just take a few minutes."

"I'll go with you, Ernie," Dad suggested.

"You don't have to, Dad," Ernesto said. Brutus was jumping and straining at the improvised leash, but Ernesto was strong enough to hold him. Father and son set off for Bluebird Street.

As they walked, Ernesto recalled a time when Naomi, a slight girl, had tried to control the dog. She had gotten his chain wrapped around her arm, and the chain had left a nasty bruise. Whenever Ernesto thought of Naomi, he felt a deep yearning. Her beautiful face came to mind, and he got goose bumps. "Naomi isn't afraid of Brutus like her mom is, but she can't control him," Ernesto mentioned to his Dad.

"You like Naomi, eh *mi hijo?*" Dad asked as they turned the corner toward the Martinez house.

"Yeah Dad," Ernesto admitted, "but she's got this creep boyfriend, Clay Aguirre. She told me she loves him. Is that crazy or what? He isn't even nice to her."

Brutus was jumping and straining at the rope. When he escaped from the Martinez yard, he was in his glory. He enjoyed the newfound freedom—chasing squirrels, cats, anything that moved, even leaves. Now they had taken his freedom away. They neared a bunch of pigeons on the sidewalk, and Brutus lunged at them eagerly. The pigeons escaped in a flutter of feathers.

"I knew Felix Martinez when I was a kid around here," Dad confided, grimacing. "I'm not surprised he brings a dog into the house to terrify his wife."

They turned onto Bluebird Street and headed for the green stucco house. "They still live there, eh?" Dad asked.

When they drew close to the house, they heard loud yelling and cursing. Ernesto figured Mr. Martinez was blaming his wife for letting the dog get out.

"You moron!" Felix Martinez was yelling. "Why did you leave the door open?"

Zack Martinez, Naomi's older brother, spotted Ernesto and his father coming with Brutus. "Hey Dad!" he shouted. "Some guys are comin' with the dog now."

The front door swung open, and there stood Felix Martinez, his face flushed with fury. He looked at Ernesto's father. "I know you," he noted. "You're Luis Sandoval. I heard you came back to the *barrio*."

"Brutus was in our yard," Ernesto stated.

Martinez grabbed the rope leash from Ernesto and said, "Thanks a lot. My idiot wife left the door open, and he just took off. He's wanting to run all the time." He smiled a little, "Come on in for some beer, you guys. I sure do appreciate you getting Brutus back to me."

"No thanks," Luis Sandoval declined. "It's too early in the morning to be drinking. Besides, Ernie and I need to get to Chavez High."

Zack Martinez was sitting on the corner of a chair, drinking from a can of beer. He was probably seventeen. Ernesto hadn't see him at Chavez. Maybe he dropped out, Ernesto thought, or maybe he already graduated. He was trying to mask his shock at the open beer can.

Linda Martinez stood in the darkened hallway, barely visible. She shrank back when the pit bull came in.

"I always keep Brutus on a leash or behind a locked gate," Martinez asserted. "These wimps around here see a pit bull, and they go nuts. He's a nice dog, though. Don't you think he's a nice dog, Sandoval?"

"I guess so," Ernesto's father admitted.

"See, *stupid?*" Felix Martinez glared at his wife. "Nobody's scared of Brutus but you. This guy and his kid didn't have a problem with the dog." He turned his attention back to the Sandovals. "She left the door open. That's the kind of an idiot she is."

Zack laughed. He almost choked on his beer. He thought what his father was saying about his mother was funny. Ernesto was glad Naomi wasn't here to see this ugly spectacle, but then she probably saw enough anyway.

Ernesto saw annoyance turn to anger in his father's eyes. "Felix, what other people do is none of my business, but stop it. Enough! *Basta!*"

Martinez looked puzzled. "What? What's up, man? What are you talking about?"

"Man," Dad told him, "you oughtn't be calling your wife names, especially not in front of the boy there. That's his *mother* man. So she made a mistake and let the dog get out. Okay. But you need to respect her. She's your wife. You don't throw words like 'stupid' and 'moron' around. She's your woman, Felix."

Felix Martinez grinned scornfully. "You were always weird, Sandoval. I remember when we were kids, you were this Goody Two–shoes getting offended by everything. Well, lissen up. Me and Linda been together for thirty years, and she ain't goin' nowhere and neither am I. We don't need no scolding from some sissy guy who probably sleeps with his tie on." Then he added, "But, hey, thanks for bringing the dog back. That was real nice.

You sure you and the boy don't want a cold beer?"

"We don't drink," Dad snapped.

Martinez shrugged and closed the door. As the Sandovals turned and walked away, they heard him yelling. "See what you caused, dummy? You embarrassed me in front of that jerk, Sandoval. He thinks he's got the right to lecture me because he's a teacher. Well, that don't cut no ice with me. I'm a heavy equipment operator. That's a man's job."

Dad shook his head as they headed for home. "Martinez was a bully when we were kids," Dad explained. "He'd pick on the younger kids, me and my friends. He'd give us a hard time. It makes me sick how he talks to his wife. In front of that boy too. Did you see the boy laughing? He's growing up thinking that's how you treat girls and women. He thinks that's how families work. When he gets married, it'll be the same way. It just goes on and on like a stream of polluted water. I hear some of the guys at Chavez yelling at their girlfriends," Dad lamented. "They don't even have to be mad. They call them these ugly names, and the girls just take it."

Ernesto thought about Naomi Martinez, the girl he cared so much about. Her boyfriend, Clay Aguirre, called her names sometimes. She was a smart, beautiful girl, but she took the abuse from him.

When they were almost home, Naomi rode up to them on her bike. "Hi Ernie. Hi. Mr. Sandoval," she called, stopping her bike and standing next to them. "I'm on my way to school. It's a great morning to ride a bike. I rode all the way down to the ravine where the lake is. It's filled with ducks, and I saw some Canada geese arriving for the winter."

"I've seen them too," Dad replied. "They're very impressive birds."

Naomi looked from Ernesto to his father, sensing that something was wrong. "Where you guys coming from?" she asked.

"Brutus got out, and he was in our yard chasing our cat," Ernesto explained.

11

Naomi paled. "Oh my gosh! He didn't hurt the cat, did he?" she gasped.

"No," Ernesto assured her, "she ran up into the pepper tree. I don't think Brutus was trying to hurt her anyway. He just wanted to play. Me and Dad caught him and brought him home."

"I hope Brutus didn't scare your mom and your little sisters, Ernie," Naomi said, still looking concerned. "I mean, a pit bull . . . Oh Ernie, I'm so sorry that happened. Mr. Sandoval, I'm sorry you had to round up our dog." Naomi was one of the best students in Dad's American history class. And he was Naomi's favorite teacher in the whole school.

Dad smiled and told her, "There wasn't any problem. I think my little girls enjoyed the excitement."

"Brutus didn't try to bite anybody, did he?" Naomi asked.

"No, no," Dad responded. "He's not a bad dog. Just a big unruly puppy. He'll settle down."

"Mr. Sandoval," Naomi said, "you have no idea how scared my mom is of that dog. I've been hoping Dad would trade him in for a smaller dog, maybe a cocker spaniel or even a terrier."

"That would be good," Dad agreed. "But I wouldn't count on it happening."

Naomi nodded, realizing that her teacher understood the situation better than she hoped he did. She was embarrassed by what must be going through his mind. She said nothing else and rode off toward the school.

When they were almost home, Ernesto made an observation. "The problem in that house isn't the pit bull, Dad. I wouldn't want a pit bull myself, but the problem isn't the dog."

"I hear you, *mi hijo*," Dad concurred ruefully.

When they got home, Mom was at the computer. "You guys will be late for school if you don't hurry. Did everything go all right over at the Martinez house?" she asked.

13

"Yeah, Mom," Ernesto replied. He didn't feel like saying more. Mom did not like the Martinez family anyway. She never came right out and said so. But she wished Ernesto was not trying to start a relationship with Naomi Martinez. Ernesto could just tell she felt that way. Mom thought Naomi had to be scarred from growing up in that home.

"A lot of people would have called animal control if there was a pit bull loose in their yard," Mom remarked. "The Martinezes are lucky that didn't happen. A dog that strong could hurt a small child just being playful." Mom turned her attention back to the computer.

"Whatcha doin', Mom?" Katalina asked. "You checking out Facebook?"

"No, I'm looking for an agent," Mom answered.

Dad and Ernesto both stopped in their tracks. Maria Vasquez had wanted to be a writer when she was a teenager. Her plan was to major in English in college and then become a writer. While she was still a teenager, several of her short stories and articles had been published in youth magazines. But then she fell in love with Luis Sandoval, and all her energies were directed toward getting him through college and launched as a teacher.

Mom laughed. "Look at the two of you staring at me," she exclaimed. "It's almost as if I told you I'd just had contact with aliens coming off a UFO. You think maybe I want to join a rock band, and I need an agent? No, sillies, I am reviving an old dream."

"I bet you're writing something," Dad ventured. "I bet those wonderful dreams you used to have about being an author are springing back into life. *Mi querida,* that's wonderful."

Mom giggled. "I was thinking. *Abuela* Lena will probably be coming to live with us, and she'll spend a lot of time with the girls. Then my baby is coming." The Sandovals were expecting their fourth child. "So I'll

—

have time while he is sleeping. I'm thinking of writing a picture book. All sorts of plots are buzzing around in my mind."

"This is wonderful!" Dad exclaimed.

"Maybe nothing will come of it, of course," Mrs. Sandoval admitted. "Who knows? My mom and dad were so proud when I got those little stories published years ago. They were disappointed that I didn't go to college. Then they thought maybe I would become a writer. But I stopped writing. I got busy with the kids. If I ever wrote a book, and it was actually published, my parents would be so happy!"

"You know what?" Katalina suggested, having overheard the last part of the conversation. "You could write a book about a pit bull, Mama. He could be a big, noisy pit bull that everybody was a scared of. But in his heart he could be a nice dog. He could be so nice that pretty soon everybody liked him. He could be so nice that nobody was afraid of him anymore. He could be like Brutus!"

Mom laughed. "That's not a bad idea, Katalina. Trouble is I *am* still a little afraid of Brutus."

"Calico is too," Juanita chimed in. "She wouldn't come down from the pepper tree even after he was gone."

"Calico could be in your story too, Mama," Katalina continued. "She could learn to be best friends with Brutus."

"I don't think Calico *ever* wants to be best friends with Brutus," Juanita commented.

Ernesto got a call on his cell phone, and he went into his bedroom to take it. He recognized it was from Naomi. As Mr. Sandoval left the house, he urged Ernesto to make the call short or he'd be late for school.

"Hey Naomi, what's up?" he asked when he was alone.

"Ernie, I hate to bother you," Naomi said. "But I need to go visit a friend at the hospital after school this afternoon. Would there be any chance of you taking me?"

Ernesto was puzzled. He knew Naomi's mother didn't drive, but she always rode with Clay Aguirre after school. Why didn't she ask him? But Ernesto had no intention of turning down a golden opportunity to spend some time with Naomi. "No problem," he replied quickly. "I'll go to my Volvo in the parking lot right after my last class and meet you there."

"Oh Ernie, you're an angel!" she cried. "I'll see you at school. Are you on your way?"

"Yeah," Ernesto answered, hurrying out to the Volvo. He'd be thinking about taking Naomi to the hospital to see her friend all day. He'd try to concentrate on *Macbeth* in Ms. Hunt's English class and on the problems of global warming in Mr. Escalante's science class. But he would be thinking of Naomi being in the car with him after school. It wouldn't be a date, of course. He was just doing her a favor. But riding around with her would sort of *feel* like a date: Ernesto at the wheel, a beautiful girl

18

he liked beside him. It could hardly get any better than that until the time, he hoped, when it really *would* be a date.

After classes ended, Ernesto raced to the parking lot to avoid any chance of missing the connection. Naomi biked up to him within minutes.

"Hey, Ernie!" she called. She detached the front wheel of her bike, and Ernie loaded it and rest of the bike into the trunk of his Volvo.

"This is so nice of you, Ernie," she told him. "I promised Tessie I'd come see her. Clay drives me lots of places where I need to go because I don't have my driver's license yet. But he was so busy. He's struggling in a couple classes. He's always worried he's gonna slip below a C average and lose his eligibility to play football. He just loves football so much."

"Poor Clay," Ernesto thought to himself. "Maybe the dude shouldn't sit in the back of the classroom and look at magazines instead of paying attention. Maybe then he'd do better." Mr. Escalante never caught those *bobos* in the back with their magazines, but Clay didn't get away with it in English class. Even then, the guy wasn't very smart. Even paying attention, he still had a problem understanding stuff like Shakespeare.

"My brother Zack would've driven me," Naomi went on, "but he's busy fixing his Honda. He's putting in a new fuel pump. I wouldn't even ask my dad. He works so hard all day that when he comes home, he just wants to collapse in his easy chair and . . . you know, drink his beer. I guess most guys his age do that."

Ernesto made no comment.

Naomi turned toward Ernesto, her amazing violet eyes like jewels. "Thanks loads for this, Ernie," she thanked him. "Tessie really needs her friends with her right now."

CHAPTER TWO

Uh Ernie," Naomi began as they neared the hospital, "Would you do me a favor and not mention it to Clay that I hitched a ride with you today? I mean, he can be so insecure. I prefer he thought Dad or my brother drove me. I don't want to put more pressure on Clay when he's worrying about his classes and stuff."

"No problem," Ernesto agreed. "I don't talk to the guy anyway. I mean, we're not friends. He's in English with me, but like we got nothing in common."

Still, Ernesto was a little surprised and even disgusted that Naomi would make such a request. She was afraid that Clay Aguirre would be mad that a classmate—a guy—drove her to the hospital to see a friend. What was that all about? Ernesto felt like upchucking when he thought that a lovely girl like her had to be nervous about such an innocent act.

As he drove into the visitors parking area at the hospital, Ernesto asked, "Is your friend seriously sick, Naomi?"

"She was injured in a terrible accident," Naomi explained. "For a while it looked like she might not live, but now she's getting better. Tessie Zamora is on the cheerleading team with me, Ernie. She's a wonderful friend. She's so beautiful and upbeat. About a month ago, right before you came to Chavez, she and another girl, Claudia, they were crossing Caldwell Street late in the day at dusk. A car came along and hit Tessie. Claudia wasn't struck, but Tessie was thrown about ten feet. Her right leg was broken, and she was in a coma for about two days. They were afraid she had brain damage or something. It was so awful. I've known Tessie since we were little kids together, and she's like a sister to me."

Naomi was quiet for a few moments as Ernesto looked for a parking spot. Then she continued. "Poor Tessie! She's been stuck in that hospital for so long. I think she's coming out pretty soon. She gets so creeped out just lying there. Her mother and father visit every night, but they both work during the afternoon. I try to visit her every chance I get. The other cheerleaders have been great too. Rosalie Rivas comes every single day. She's been awesome."

"How did it happen?" Ernesto wondered out loud. "The accident, I mean. Were the girls in a crosswalk?"

Just then, a boy on a skateboard shot out in front of Ernesto's Volvo. Because he was going slowly in the hospital parking lot, Ernesto had no trouble stopping. But if he had been speeding, as some cars do even in the parking area, he might have hit the boy.

"Just like that," Naomi remarked sadly. "Claudia and Tessie were jabbering away.

They just dashed across the street in the middle of the block. They never saw the car coming, and the driver didn't see them until it was too late."

"Oh man!" Ernesto moaned. "I bet the guy who hit her felt terrible. I think I'd have a nervous breakdown or something if I hurt somebody with my car."

"Ernie," Naomi replied, "we don't even know who the driver was, whether it was a man or a woman or anything. The car didn't stop. It just kept going. I guess the driver got scared or something. One witness sort of described the car, but it wasn't a very good description. The police are still looking for the driver, but the trail is pretty cold. It probably wasn't even the driver's fault because Tessie and Claudia were jaywalking. But not stopping, that's hit-and-run. That's a felony. It's just so terrible, to leave someone lying in the street, maybe dying, and just drive away."

"That's awful," Ernesto agreed. Ernesto had taken drivers ed, but he learned the most from driving with his father on mornings when there was no traffic. Dad stressed that, when you drive, you have to be scanning both sides of the road. You have to be looking for that kid chasing a baseball, looking for the driver who doesn't plan to stop for a red light. But the thought of hitting someone and then driving off was almost too much for Ernesto to imagine.

"Whoever hit Tessie and then took off must have panicked," Naomi surmised. "I feel sorry for them. How can they live with themselves?"

Ernesto and Naomi walked into the hospital and rode the elevator to the third floor. "You want me to wait in the visitor's lounge while you go see your friend, Naomi?" Ernesto asked.

"It'd be nice if you came with me, Ernie," she suggested. "Poor Tessie would love another visitor even if it's somebody she doesn't know. She's so lonely. If you wouldn't mind, that is . . . It would

25

really lift her spirits to see a cute guy like you."

Ernesto felt the temperature of his face go up a few degrees. Any compliment from Naomi surely improved his day, even if it was just a casual comment designed to make him feel good. "I wouldn't mind, Naomi," replied. "I'd be happy to come with you."

Naomi led the way into the room, which Tessie shared with an elderly woman who had just had hip surgery. The divider curtain was pulled across the room, and the woman was watching television.

"Hi Tessie," Naomi said softly, giving the girl a hug and a kiss. "This is my real good friend from school, Ernesto Sandoval. He and his family just moved down from LA. His father is the best history teacher I've ever had. Ernie drove me down here today."

Tessie was a light-skinned Hispanic girl with reddish brown hair. She was very pretty, especially when she smiled, which she was doing now. "Hi Ernesto. You're pretty cute," she remarked. "I'm glad you moved down here. You'll make Chavez High nicer."

Ernesto blushed a little. He had only known Tessie for two minutes, but he liked her. "Thanks," he mumbled.

Tessie Zamora looked at Naomi. "You said this cute guy was your real good friend, Naomi. Does that mean . . . ? Could it possibly mean . . . ?" she asked.

Naomi laughed. "No. Me and Clay are still together. You *know* that's not going to change. But Ernie *is* a very special friend. He's quite a guy actually."

"Oh," Tessie said. She sounded as if she thought breaking up with Clay would be good news. Ernesto wondered whether most of Naomi's friends felt the same way. Why couldn't she get it?

Naomi changed the subject. "How are you feeling, Tessie?" she asked, sitting down on one of the chairs Ernesto pulled out for her. Ernesto sat in the other chair.

27

The chairs weren't very comfortable. Perhaps it was the hospital's way of hinting that visitors shouldn't stay long.

"Okay," Tessie responded. "I'm doing okay. I'm getting a lot of physical therapy. When I leave the hospital, I'll have to use crutches for a while. I'll probably need a wheelchair too for when I go back to school. What I want more than anything in the world is just to go home. Rosie was just here, and she promised to push my wheelchair all over Chavez High. She's such a sweetheart. She's here like every single day. I mean, we were close before, but now we're really close. I'll just *never* forget how nice she's been."

"We'll all help you get around Chavez, Tessie," Naomi offered.

"Oh, I miss school so much," Tessie continued. "Not the classes, but my friends. I never realized how wonderful it was to just go to Chavez every day and hang out with my friends. I miss our lunches . . . I miss cheerleading and the games . . . Oh,

Naomi, how could me and Claudia have been so stupid to just run across a busy street in the middle of the block when it was getting dark!"

Tessie had asked herself that question over and over since the accident. One stupid decision, and she was going through all this pain and loneliness. "I keep thinking how perfect my life was, Naomi, before all this," Tessie lamented. "I mean, I'd get one little zit and I'd be like 'Oh, woe is me!' Now I wouldn't mind if every day was a bad hair day, and I got a big zit on my nose!"

"You'll be good as new when the leg heals," Ernesto assured her. "There was a girl in my high school in Los Angeles who had this really bad ski trip. She broke her leg in three places. But in a few months she was fine. You'll heal really fast, Tessie, I know you will." Ernesto smiled at the girl.

Tessie beamed as she looked at Naomi. "Girl, he's so sweet and so cute! Are you sure . . . ?" she asked.

"Yeah, I'm stuck on Clay," Naomi replied, laughing.

Ernesto felt sorry for Tessie and what she had gone through. "Thanks for the compliments," he acknowledged. "I'm not sure they fit me but . . ."

"When I'm all healed and normal, Ernie," Tessie asked, "promise me you'll take me to Hortencia's for her super chicken *enchiladas*. That will give me something to look forward to."

"Sure thing," Ernesto agreed. "I can do that. It'll be my pleasure."

The three kids sat in a few moments of silence. Ernesto wasn't sure what else to say.

"Mom and Dad come every night," Tessie spoke up. "Both of them work hard all day, and I feel so guilty to be putting them through this. All because of my stupid mistake."

Naomi turned to Ernesto. "Tessie has such great parents. They just love her so much. You should have seen them when

Tessie was brought in here . . . just looking at their faces made your heart want to break."

"Yeah," Tessie added. "It's just me and my brother, and he's fighting over in the Gulf. My folks worry about him a lot. They didn't need this. Dad told me last night that they still don't have a clue about the car that hit me. It's supposed to be a dark car, probably a Honda, but there's like a million of those around. It was wrong of the driver not to stop, but the accident was my fault."

Naomi reached in her purse, pulled out a get-well card, and held it out toward Tessie. It was folded over several times to fit in all the signatures. "The kids wanted to sign another card, Tessie. We're all missing you so much."

There were already several cards on the little table, as well as balloons and flowers. Tessie took the new card and laughed. "Look at what Carmen wrote. 'I promised God if you got home real soon, I'd try to stop talking so much.' "

31

"When you get home, we'll have a big party at your house, Tessie," Naomi promised. "We'll bring everything so you guys don't have to worry about a thing. We'll even decorate."

Naomi leaned over and gave Tessie a hug and a kiss. "Love you, Tessie," she told her.

Tessie saw Ernesto stand up. He and Naomi were ready to go. "I don't suppose it's possible to get a hug and a kiss from that handsome dude," Tessie asked.

Ernesto grinned and bent down, hugging and kissing the girl. He brushed a kiss across her soft cheek.

"Wow!" Tessie exclaimed. "That chicken *enchilada* date still stands. Right, Ernie?"

"You can count on it," Ernesto replied.

As Naomi and Ernesto walked down the corridor to the elevators, Naomi said, "You're wonderful, Ernie. You can't imagine how you lifted that girl's spirits. You're just what she needed this afternoon."

"She seems like a really nice girl," Ernesto remarked.

"She is," Naomi affirmed. "You know, it's always Tessie Zamora running the show when there's a drive for some charity. Sometimes she's helping families get a turkey dinner during the holidays. Other times she's bringing brown bags to the homeless or blankets for the poor kids in TJ when the weather gets cold. Ever since we were kids, she's reached out to help people."

Naomi was reflective for a few moments and then continued speaking. "I remember one Christmas when she was about twelve, she told her parents not to buy her anything, but instead to let her buy some toys for the kids who don't have anything. Her parents were just blown away. And then on Christmas week, Tessie and some of us went down to pass out the toys and food baskets. None of it would have happened if she hadn't started it. We passed out toys and a lot of nonperishable food. And we passed out warm blankets.

Some of those people in the ravine were sleeping outside without even a blanket to keep them warm. They covered themselves with old newspapers. Tessie is so special."

The elevator doors opened, and they stepped inside it. Naomi could not stop talking about her friend. "When the accident happened, we all said the same thing. 'Not Tessie. It shouldn't be Tessie. That's so unfair.' And when she pulled through, it was like a miracle. The doctors thought she had brain damage and internal injuries, but it turned out to be only a concussion and a real badly broken leg. She needed a couple of operations and therapy in between. They couldn't let her go until the bones were totally set."

"That's great," Ernesto responded, very impressed. Now outside the hospital building, he led the way toward his Volvo. "I meant it about taking her out for chicken *enchiladas* at Hortencia's."

"You're such a sweetheart," Naomi told him.

CHAPTER TWO

Ernesto opened the car door for Naomi, and then he came around to the driver's side and got in. He thought to himself, "But not such a sweetheart as to win your heart, girl. You say nice things to me. But you're in love with Clay Aguirre, a creep who doesn't even know how to treat a girl."

Ernesto could tell that Tessie didn't like Clay either. Nobody who saw him for what he was liked him. Naomi was looking at him through the rose-colored glasses of love.

"So," Ernesto said as they drove from the hospital, "how's Brutus doing?"

"Oh," Naomi responded, "Dad is really careful now about locking him in so he doesn't get out in the neighborhood again. It was really lucky that he ran into *your* yard. Pit bulls are really under attack. I read in the newspaper that the military have banned all pit bull–type dogs from all their bases and stuff. There's one state—Ohio I think—they've branded pit bulls vicious, and the owners have to carry big insurance

35

policies. It's not fair, 'cause not all pit bulls are mean and dangerous. Brutus is really kinda sweet. I hope my father thanked you and your dad enough when you brought him home."

"Yeah, he thanked us," Ernesto told us. "He invited us in for beers. But Dad doesn't drink, and I don't either."

"I wish my dad didn't drink," Naomi remarked. "Or my brothers. Zack doesn't drink as much as Dad, but he drinks too much. And sometimes I think he drives the car when he shouldn't. You know, sometimes we have a family gathering or we go tailgating down at the stadium when the Chargers are home. Then the guys are all drinking, and it just changes everything. They're not as nice as when they're sober. They remember all the old grudges and stuff."

"I know what you're saying," Ernesto agreed. "We got a couple cousins who drink in our family, and somebody always drinks a little too much at holidays and stuff. They remember a grudge they have with somebody, and pretty soon there's a fight."

Ernesto shook his head. He wished he had the nerve to ask Naomi if she wanted to stop for a mocha or something to eat on the way home. But he didn't want to make her think he considered this a date. He did her a favor driving her to the hospital to see her friend, and that was all it was. Ernesto didn't want to overstep the bounds. He didn't want Naomi to think he was hitting on her when she already had a boyfriend.

"I went to a party the other night at Carmen Ibarra's house," Ernesto told her. "It was so much fun. They had a guy there singing and playing the guitar. Oscar Perez. Carmen's mom danced up a storm in this red dress. I was amazed. I was hoping you'd show up, Naomi. You would have had a ball."

A faintly sad look came to Naomi's face. "I like Carmen a lot, but her father has a problem with Clay. He won't let Clay

37

come to any of their parties or anything, and that rules me out too. I won't come without Clay. I'm not criticizing Carmen's dad or anything, Ernie, but he's uh . . . *different*. He runs a tight ship. He wears that plastic sheriff's badge, and he's not afraid to bust somebody. He won't let dopers or gangbangers come to Carmen's parties, even though Clay isn't into any of that. I can't see what Mr. Ibarra's problem with Clay is. Sometimes Clay gets a little rowdy but . . . nothing serious."

"Well, I wish you'd been there, Naomi," Ernesto said, "because it was a lot of fun. The food was great, and the music was awesome. I'm betting that guy Perez ends up singing in Vegas or somewhere big."

They neared the Martinez house then. Ernesto was sorry the drive was over. Even though this wasn't really a date, he enjoyed being with Naomi, just the two of them in the car talking.

As Ernesto pulled into the driveway, Naomi asked, "Want to come in, Ernie?

Have a soda or something? I think Mom made some cookies. She makes these little butterscotch cookies that are really good."

Ernesto parked the Volvo. But before he could get out of the car and walk into the house with Naomi, he heard angry voices inside the house. A man was cursing. He sounded very drunk. He was slurring his words. Ernesto heard no other voices, but he did hear the dog barking. Ernesto sat at the wheel staring straight ahead.

"I guess I better go home," he said. "I got some homework to do for English, Naomi. You know how Ms. Hunt is. She wants all the stuff she assigns done or else." Ernesto tried to laugh and make a joke of it, but his words sounded hollow.

Naomi looked deeply embarrassed. "Ernie, thanks again for driving me to see Tessie," she thanked him. "It really meant a lot to Tessie and to me."

"Sure, anytime," Ernesto replied. Then he turned in the seat and looked at Naomi. "Everything gonna be okay in there?"

"Oh yeah, sure," Naomi assured him. "Dad's in a bad mood, that's all. He'll be going to bed soon. He hurt his back on the job, and, you know, that can put anybody in a bad mood. Dad has a very hard job, you know. Physically hard. He's uh . . . not a kid anymore. He's almost fifty. Your dad is much younger. My oldest brother is twenty . . . you know . . ." Her voice trailed off.

Naomi got out of the car, and Ernesto popped the trunk. They took the two pieces of the bike out of the trunk and laid them on the grass. Naomi smiled at Ernesto, but she looked tense. Before Ernesto even started the car, he heard Felix Martinez yell at his daughter. "Where you been?" Then Brutus started barking so loudly that Ernesto couldn't hear anymore. He backed slowly out of the driveway. He was glad he didn't live in this house on Bluebird Street. He was sorry Naomi did.

CHAPTER THREE

Cesar Chavez High School had a big football game against archrival Wilson on Friday night. Ernesto Sandoval liked football, even though he didn't play. The thought of going to a game where Clay Aguirre would be playing made him sick. But his friend Dom Reynosa was on the team too, and Ernesto wanted to be there for him. The Chavez Cougars were having a pretty good season, led by their quarterback, a big guy named Fernando Sanchez.

The game was tied when Sanchez threw a pass to Clay Aguirre, who tipped ball into the air—and into the hands of a Wilson Wolverine. Interception! The Wolverine scooted with the ball into the Cougar end zone, putting Wilson ahead. Wilson then failed to make the extra point. The Cougars were losing by a touchdown.

Ernesto saw the anguish on Naomi's face. She couldn't bear the thought that Clay's mistake could cost the team the game. And it looked that way until Sanchez threw a touchdown pass to another receiver with just sixteen seconds on the clock. With four seconds remaining, the Cougars made the extra point and squeaked out a one-point victory. The Chavez bleachers exploded in joy.

Fernando jumped and hopped off the field, pumping his fist in the air. One of the cheerleaders, Rosalie Rivas, blew him a kiss.

Game over! The teams mingled on the field, shaking hands. Then the players drifted toward their sidelines to collect their share of hugs, kisses, and handshakes.

Ernesto was glad that Dom Reynosa scored one of the two touchdowns that won the game. Clay Aguirre surely didn't do himself proud in the game, and that thought didn't bother Ernesto. In fact, Ernesto was glad he didn't have to watch Clay strutting around the field. He always made a fool of himself when he scored. But, in spite of his dismal performance, Naomi hurried to him and gave him a hug.

Ernesto turned away, looking for a friendly face. He left the stands with Abel Ruiz and Carlos Negrete. Both Carlos and Dom had been taggers and gang wannabes. Then Ernesto's father worked with the art department at Chavez to get them working on a mural for the side of the science building. The two guys were so busy making their masterpiece of Cesar Chavez among the farmworkers that they had even gotten interested again in staying in school and maybe even graduating.

"How's the mural going, man?" Ernesto asked Carlos.

"We got it all designed out on paper, and we start the outline on the wall next week," Carlos answered.

"It's gonna feature a scene from March 1966," Dom added. "That's when Chavez led the grape strike in Delano. Chavez went on a fast to support the grape workers to get better wages and working conditions. We're painting American and Mexican flags in the scene, 'cause that's what the strikers carried."

"Yeah," Carlos went on, "and we're painting this banner of Our Lady of Guadalupe 'cause Chavez always carried that at the head of his march. And we're doing a big black eagle, the symbol of the United Farm Workers. It's gonna be spectacular man!"

"We got the faces of some of the people who supported Chavez in the mural too," Dom added. "Senator Robert Kennedy, Coretta Scott King . . . I'm tellin' you man, the TV stations are gonna do a piece on the mural when we're done. We're gonna put Cesar Chavez High School on the map, dude."

"Sounds great," Ernesto said. He was so glad Abel Ruiz suggested the mural, and he was proud of his father for running with the idea. Ernesto turned to Dom, "You did a pretty good job on the football field tonight, man. Without your touchdown we would've lost."

Dom grinned. "I guess old Fernando saved the day, though, after that jerk Aguirre coughed up the ball to Wilson."

"I don't know Fernando," Ernesto asked. "What's he like?"

"He's got an ego as big as the state of California man," Dom responded. "He's not as creepy as Aguirre, but he's no prize."

Abel Ruiz joined the conversation. "I got a class with Fernando Sanchez. He's the biggest cheat I ever saw. He takes reports off the Net and turns them in as his own work. Old Mr. Castillo doesn't know the difference. If Fernando had Ms. Hunt, he'd get busted in two minutes. But Mr. Castillo's been teaching since the Civil War, I think, and he doesn't even know what's out there on the Net."

"Why doesn't somebody tip the teacher off?" Dom asked.

Abel laughed. "And get the star of the Chavez Cougars busted for cheating? He'd lose his eligibility to play football, and there goes our chances to be in the division playoffs man. How important is cheating when we're talking about the championships?"

"Yeah," Carlos affirmed. "Fernando is untouchable. He's a junior but he's almost eighteen. He's had his driver's license for a long time, and he's had a couple DUIs. Nothing happens to the dude."

"How's that possible?" Ernesto asked. "You get a DUI, and they come down hard on you. Especially a young driver. He's underage."

"Fernando's family pulled some strings," Carlos explained. "They got a good lawyer. Most of the kids who go to Chavez are poor or lower middle, you know, but Fernando's folks got a lotta green."

"That stinks!" Dom remarked. "Makes you think the whole system is rotten. Some drunken dude shouldn't walk after a DUI just because his parents got money."

Abel laughed. "Dude, you just figuring it out that justice ain't the same for a homie from Sparrow Street and a dude with clout? If I got caught driving drunk, they'd have me cuffed so fast my head would spin. It's the same all over, man. Some athlete down in Florida killed a guy in a drunk driving accident. They lost the test results, so the pro walked, free as one of those Florida pelicans."

"I wish I'd see the dude cheating in class," Dom declared darkly. "I'd rat him out."

"Yeah," Carlos asserted, "and watch the Chavez Cougars go down in flames this season! What'd you be doin' man is running for the most unpopular dude on campus."

When Ernesto got home, his mother was working on the computer. She was on fire with her newfound enthusiasm for her old writing dreams.

"You working on your book, Mom?" Ernesto asked her. Mom had been happy to stand in Dad's shadow for a lot of years. But now that she was dreaming on her own again, Ernesto was happy and so was Dad.

"Yep," Mom replied. "It's going pretty good. I've been talking with an agent, a lady up in North County. Her name is Janet, and she said to send her a proposal for my book. She sounds really nice. We hit it off right away. I'm kind of excited, Ernie."

"Way to go, Mom," Ernesto responded. Then he went looking for his father. He found him in the backyard just staring up at the sky. "What's up, Dad?" he asked.

"What a night, huh, Ernie?" Dad mused. "Look at those stars. They're so beautiful they give me goose bumps."

Ernesto glanced upward, but he had other thoughts on his mind.

"Dad, do you catch kids cheating much in your classes?" Ernesto asked.

"When I first started teaching in LA, I had some problems, but now I try to outsmart them," Dad answered. When I give those multiple-choice, true-false tests, I use different tests on alternating rows. And I use the essay test a lot, and it's hard to cheat there. Why do you ask, Ernie?"

"Some of the guys were talking about how there's cheating going on in a few classes," Ernesto explained. "Guys taking stuff off the Net and turning it in as their work. Stuff like that."

"Yeah, I heard that too," Dad said. "Sometimes a teacher gets careless. I don't like to assign much take-home work. Parents or older siblings do too much of the work, or else the kids buy stuff on the Net. I like to have the work done in class so I really know what the kid can do on his own."

"If you know somebody is cheating," Ernesto continued slowly, "like what should you do?"

Luis Sandoval turned and looked at his son intently. "Do you know a kid who's cheating, Ernie?"

"Not firsthand, but I heard stuff," Ernesto responded.

"Well, if you don't know for sure yourself, you can't be spreading rumors," Dad advised. "But if you actually see cheating taking place in your classroom, tell the teacher. Cheating makes a mockery out of the whole educational process. Okay son?"

Ernesto smiled. "Yeah, Dad, I get it."

Now he looked up at the stars too. "Mom's working on her book," he mentioned. "She seems really excited. Wouldn't it be great if something came of that?"

Dad smiled too. "It would be wonderful. Your mom surely deserves it."

Ernesto was on his own computer later that night when he got to thinking about Tessie Zamora. What a nice, sweet girl she was. How could somebody have struck her and left her in the street without stopping? What kind of a person would do that? Ernesto could not imagine leaving even a wounded animal in the street and not trying to help.

Ernesto pulled up recent news stories on the computer, and he found the item about the hit-and-run accident that injured Tessie.

"Chavez High Student Critically Injured," the headline read. Ernesto went into the article.

Teresa Zamora, a sixteen-year-old student at Cesar Chavez High School, was crossing Caldwell Street around six p.m. Wednesday night when she was struck in midblock by an automobile. The driver did not stop and now is being sought for felony hit-and-run. Witnesses described the car as a dark sedan, possibly a Honda Civic. Zamora is being treated for head injuries, internal injuries, and a broken leg. She is a cheerleader at Chavez High, and her friends immediately erected a small shrine of candles, teddy bears, and cards as they prayed for her recovery.

A dark Honda Civic? Ernesto had seen such a car in the *barrio* recently. Zack Martinez, Naomi's brother, was fixing his fuel pump on a dark Honda Civic. But there had to be many such cars. The model was very

popular. Ernesto wondered whether a
Chavez student hit Tessie. That would
make the accident all the more terrible. The
driver, he figured, was probably a stranger
driving through town. Caldwell was the
street that ran north and south next to
Tremayne. A lot of stores lined the street.

Yet Ernesto kept thinking about Zack
Martinez's Honda. Naomi was fretting
about the fact that her brother drank too
much. She even said that he drove after he
had too much to drink. Could Zack have
gone down Caldwell buzzed and hit Tessie?
Ernesto had never taken a close look at the
Honda in the Martinez front yard. He
wondered whether the car had front-end
damage. You couldn't hit somebody without doing some damage to your car.

At midmorning on Sunday, Ernesto
jogged over to Bluebird Street. He had been
thinking about Zack's Honda all night. In
fact, his suspicions ruined his sleep. Now
he wanted to take a quick look at the car,

hoping he wouldn't find any damage. He didn't want Naomi's brother to be the hit-and-run driver.

Ernesto had to admit to himself that, even if he found front-end damage on Zack's car, he probably wouldn't do anything about it. He couldn't make trouble for Naomi's family on the basis of just circumstantial evidence. As he neared Bluebird Street, Ernesto was hoping even harder that he wouldn't see anything suspicious. He only wanted to get out of his mind—and out of his nightmares—the horrible image of a drunken Zack Martinez running down Tessie. He wanted to convince himself that Zack had nothing to do with the accident.

When Ernesto jogged up to the Martinez house, the Honda Civic was parked in the front yard. It was unmoved from the last time Ernesto had seen it. Maybe Zack didn't have enough money for a new fuel pump, or maybe he didn't have the time to install one.

Ernesto ventured closer to the Honda: The whole front end showed a lot of damage. Some of the dents were corroded, as if they had been there for a long time. The front bumper had an especially big dent. Ernesto didn't want to believe it was made by Tessie's body being struck. A cold chill went up his spine. He turned numb.

"Hey man, what's up?" Zack asked, coming out the front door. "You want to steal my car? Be my guest. It's a piece of junk."

"Uh . . . hi Zack," Ernesto replied. "I'd like to get a car like this maybe. I just bought a Volvo, but I don't plan to keep it long. But this car looks like it's been in a few accidents."

Zack laughed. "I got it cheap. It's ready for the crusher, but it still runs. When I get the fuel pump in, it'll get me around."

"Banged up pretty bad," Ernesto noted.

"Yeah," Zack nodded, "some idiot stopped right in front of me for no reason, and I crashed into the back of his car. That's the worst damage. Guess who got charged with the accident? My old man was really steamed. Our insurance rates are going up, and he wants to take it out of my hide."

Ernesto shrugged. He wanted to believe Zack's story. It was probably true. "How's Brutus?" he asked.

"Okay I guess," Zack answered. "Ma went to visit her sister for a couple days. I think she just wanted to get away from the dog 'cause she usually don't go visiting her sister. They don't get along. But anything to get away from old Brutus. Just me and Naomi and Dad home. None of us mind the pit bull."

"Naomi's a strong girl," Ernesto commented.

"Yeah," Zack agreed. "You gotta be strong to get along with this wild bunch." Zack came closer. "Naomi said you and her visited Tessie Zamora at the hospital. How's she doing?"

"She's doing okay," Ernesto reported. "She really wants to be outta there, though." He stared at Zack to see whether he could detect guilt in his face. He didn't see any. "She thinks she'll get out next week."

"It was a fool thing she and that other chick did, just runnin' into the street like that," Zack remarked. "Tessie's an airhead, like most chicks. It burns me up when I'm driving along and somebody, usually a girl or some old woman, just steps off the curb in front of me like they own the street. Most chicks got no brains. I guess she won't be doing stuff like that again anytime soon. She had to learn the hard way." Zack was cold-blooded, like his father, Ernesto thought. Then Zack went on. "My sister is smarter than most chicks. You know, Ernie, she thinks you're a pretty cool dude."

"Yeah?" Ernesto reacted, suddenly liking Zack a little better.

"Yeah," Zack affirmed. "If she wasn't crazy 'bout that jerk Clay Aguirre, I think she'd go for you man. She's always talkin' you up, what a great guy you are. Naomi, she earns top grades in school, and I figure, of all of us, she's gonna go the farthest. Only stupid thing about her is Clay Aguirre, but what are you gonna do? Chicks are chicks."

Ernesto shrugged and said nothing. "I'm doing a lot of jogging, more since I'm on the track team at school. . . . Anyway, see you, Zack," Ernesto said before leaving.

Seeing the banged-up Honda in the Martinez yard didn't settle things in Ernesto's mind, as he'd hoped it would. But he felt pretty sure Zack wasn't the hit-and-run driver. It was a gut feeling, but Ernesto trusted it.

As Ernesto was jogging down the street, he saw another Honda coming fast. It was metallic red, a beautiful car. Ernesto recognized Fernando at the wheel. The car was going much too fast for a residential street. Skateboarders—middle schoolers—were in the street. Fernando didn't even seem to be slowing down. He came toward the boys as though he was going to crash right into

57

them if they didn't get out of his way. The kids scrambled to the curb as he approached. As Fernando tore by, he yelled at the boys, hurling insults at them. He told them to get out of the street, and he cursed them.

Ernesto continued jogging down the sidewalk. When he reached the skateboarders, he recognized one of them, Carlos Negrete's little brother, Estebán. The kid was about eleven, and he had pure hatred in his eyes.

"Did you see that *diablo*?" the boy asked Ernesto. "I'm gonna find out where he parks that car, and I'm gonna key it. I'll fix him!"

The other two boys laughed. "That was Fernando Sanchez," one of them said, "the big shot football player from Chavez High."

"I'd like to slash his tires," Estebán raged. "He come at us like we were nothin'. I think he woulda killed us all if we hadna run!"

"Yeah," the other boy fumed. "He acted like we were pigeons and he could chop us up with his car."

"I seen him runnin' into pigeons," one of the boys attested. "I seen those pigeon feathers flyin' up in a cloud. He's *loco*. He got mad 'cause there was pigeon goop all over his car."

Estebán stood up, holding his skateboard. He looked at Ernesto. "You're Ernesto Sandoval, aren't you? Carlos's friend?" he asked.

"Yeah. Carlos is a good guy," Ernesto said.

"You know that dude, Sanchez?" Estebán asked.

"No," Ernesto replied. "I just came to Chavez. I don't know many kids. I was born around here, but we been living in LA for a long time. I heard Fernando Sanchez was a bad driver, though, and he's got a big head."

"I hate him!" Estebán seethed. "I hate Sanchez! I watched the game on Friday.

59

When he made that touchdown, I was mad.
I wanted the Cougars to win, but I didn't
want him to look good. He's always drivin'
around like crazy, and sometimes he's
drunk too. I don't know why they don't put
him in jail or something. I'm gonna go to
Chavez High and find his car where it's
parked. And I'm gonna scratch marks in the
side and make it look ugly, like he is. That's
what I'm gonna do. He can't get away with
stuff . . ."

"Lissen up, *amigo*," Ernesto spoke
softly. "I hear you, and you got a right to
be mad. He came down a street where
there's houses and kids playing, and he
was driving like a madman. That's not
right. But if you vandalize his car, you'll
just get in trouble. You know what you
want to do? You got a phone that takes
pictures, right?"

"Yeah, Carlos has one," Estebán said.

"Well, you be ready," Ernesto advised.
"When you see him driving like that again,
you use your phone to prove it. Then you

and your parents take that down to the police station and tell them this guy is endangering the lives of people in the *barrio*."

"They won't do nothin'," Estebán insisted. "People complained about Sanchez before, and nothin' happens. I'm gonna key his car. I'm gonna mess it up bad. Then he'll have to get it painted again."

"What do you mean, 'get it painted again'?" Ernesto asked. "Did he just get the car painted?"

"Yeah," Estebán answered. "He got it painted about a month ago. I heard he took it to his cousin's repair shop in some other town, I think. His cousin, I guess he musta' given him a good price. I 'member 'cuz Sanchez wasn't drivin' for few days. Then someone picks him up—his cousin, I guess. Later he comes drivin' back in a red Honda, lookin' good as new. He got it painted that metallic red. He got it fixed too. It had a busted front window and stuff."

Ernesto stood there, staring at the boy. "What color was Fernando's car before he got it painted red?"

"It was like dark, dark green," the boy replied. Ernesto stiffened. What if Fernando Sanchez was the hit-and-run driver? What if he painted and fixed his car to cover the damage caused when he hit Tessie Zamora?

It was just a wild guess, Ernesto told himself. He was jumping to conclusions. The guy just happened to get a windshield fixed and a paint job done at the same time the accident happened. Maybe his windshield was cracked when he rode behind a gravel truck. Maybe he got caught in a sandstorm that busted the windshield and damaged the car's finish at the same time.

Ernesto tried to push the thought from his mind. He had to quit playing detective. The police were looking into the matter. They knew what to look for. Ernesto was just grasping at straws. The police had probably already checked out Sanchez's

Honda before it was repainted, and they cleared him. Yeah, no doubt.

Ernesto continued running, reaching the park. He was on the dirt trail meandering through the park, and he ran a little faster. He loved running on dirt trails. Running had a way of clearing your mind. When Ernesto was worried about something, like a school project, he calmed his fears by running. Ernesto found that he could master whatever project he was worried about after a run. Running gave him peace.

Ernesto expected, if he tried hard, to become excellent on the Chavez track team. He could help Coach Muñoz finally realize his dream of having a track team that had a chance of winning meets against other schools.

CHAPTER FOUR

The next Monday afternoon, Fernando Sanchez's red Honda was parked in its usual place at school. He had football practice. So by the time he arrived at his car to drive home, the lot had pretty much emptied out. The practice had gone well, and Fernando was still glowing from his winning touchdown during the last game.

But when he reached his car, his heart sank. Horrible scratches marred both car doors where someone had keyed it. Within minutes a small crowd gathered at the damaged car. The cheerleaders came, and the rest of the football team arrived to offer their sympathy.

"I just had it painted!" Fernando was screaming.

"That's rough man," Clay Aguirre offered, showing one of his rare displays of sympathy. In his heart he didn't feel too badly. He was jealous of Fernando's skill on the football field. While Clay was coughing up the ball, Fernando was getting ready for the winning touchdown. But Clay tried to be on good terms with Fernando and with the other guys on the team. Coach insisted on team members' getting along.

"I can't imagine who would do such a thing," Naomi Martinez wondered. "I mean, it's such a stupid, mindless thing to do."

"One of the creeps from Wilson musta come over and done it," Fernando guessed. "They're still boiling about us whipping them in the last seconds of that game. They were so sure they were going to win. Gotta be one of them. One of the crazy fans. Well, I'm telling you, this is not gonna stand. I'm gonna complain to coach, and he'll get on

Wilson's case. Those creeps can't come over here and do stuff like this."

Ernesto heard the commotion, and he came over. He stood there silently. He knew what had happened, but he wasn't about to rat on Estebán. He had seen the red Honda scattering the skateboarders. He had heard Estebán's bitter threats. Ernesto had no intention of turning Fernando's rage against the eleven-year-old boy.

"Can't you get somebody to just buff it and wax it so the scratches don't look so bad?" Carmen asked. "I mean, they don't look very deep."

"No *dummy*," Clay Aguirre sneered rudely. "It's gonna be a big expensive job. You can't just paper it over!"

Carmen's eyes smoked and her nostrils flared. "Don't be calling me a dummy," Carmen raged. "Aguirre. Don't forget, I'm in two of your classes, and you are the stupidest dude in both of them. The other day in history class, you wondered if the Germans were on our side in World War II against the Russians. You thought Joseph Stalin was the head of Germany. You're so dumb, Clay Aguirre, that it's amazing they let you play football. I mean, you shoulda lost your eligibility last year."

"Listen to her," Clay snarled. "She's a moron, and her old man is crazy. *Loco*! He runs around pretending to be a sheriff with a plastic badge he got out of a corn flakes carton. He oughta be in the loony bin."

"Aguirre, you got hit in the head playing football too often," Carmen snapped. "You had *poquito* brains to start with, and what little you had you left out on the playing field."

Naomi looked pained. "Carmen . . . ," she pleaded.

"I don't care!" Carmen flared. "I don't take no stuff from any dude, not especially from *bobos* like him."

Ms. Hunt was one of the teachers who remained after teaching hours in her classroom to be available to students who needed help. She heard the commotion in the parking lot and came walking up to the group. She was a pretty, well liked Anglo teacher about thirty-two years old. She never had any trouble controlling her class or with keeping the students in line.

"What's going on here?" Ms. Hunt asked.

"Somebody keyed my car man," Fernando whined. "I think some freaks from Wilson were mad we won the game last Friday, and they took it out on me 'cause I got the winning touchdown."

"Fernando," Ms. Hunt asserted, "that's pure speculation. It has never happened before. The fans from Wilson have been noisy, but they've never done any vandalism. We've beaten them, and they have beaten us. Nobody has resorted to anything ugly ever."

Two freshman girls came slowly walking up. They kept looking at one another for support.

"We kinda saw what happened, Ms. Hunt," one of them announced. "We were finishing band practice, and we saw what happened."

"Thank you for coming forward," Ms. Hunt assured them. "Please come to my classroom, and we'll talk."

"I'd like to know right now what they saw," Fernando yelled. "I want to know who did this to my car!"

"I am going to interview the girls in private," Ms. Hunt stated coldly. "We're not going to have a circus out here in the parking lot!"

In her classroom, Ms. Hunt invited the girls to sit down and to make their account.

"We saw this little boy skateboarding around the parking lot," one of the girls told Ms. Hunt. "When he got to the red car, he keyed it real fast. Then he ran away."

"He looked about ten," the other girl added. "But maybe he was older, like eleven or twelve. He sorta looked like a middle schooler."

"I've never seen him before," the first girl said. "He wore a hoodie, and he was dark."

"Me neither," the other girl confirmed. "I don't know who he is."

Ms. Hunt thanked the girls again for coming forward and dismissed them. She then poked her head out the building door and asked Fernando to come to her class-room. When they were seated, Ms. Hunt addressed Fernando.

"The girls said a little boy keyed your car. They didn't recognize him. You need to tell your parents what happened, and they'll probably file a report. And then, of course, your insurance company needs to know."

"Great!" Fernando moaned bitterly. "We got a thousand dollars deductible for that kind of thing on our insurance!"

Ernesto was buying an apple at the vending machine when Naomi came along. "Poor Fernando!" she sighed, "He spent so much to make his car look perfect less than a month ago. Now someone's ruined his car!"

"Stuff happens," Ernesto remarked.

"I heard it was a little kid who did it," Naomi went on. "Some freshman girls are telling everybody it was a little boy. Can you imagine?"

Ernesto bit into his apple. It was sweet and crispy, just the way he liked apples. "Maybe the kid had a beef with Fernando," he suggested.

"Ernie, why would a little boy have a beef with Fernando?" Naomi wondered. "It doesn't make sense."

"You never know," Ernesto commented, taking another bite of his apple.

"Ernie, you have a strange look on your face," Naomi noted. "Do you know more about this than you're saying? Fernando and Clay are really close. I know Clay would appreciate it if we could get to the bottom of this nasty prank against his friend. I'd be so happy to tell Clay what happened so he could let Fernando know."

"Oh!" Ernesto thought. "That would be wonderful. I really want to help you get in solid with good old Clay Aguirre, babe.

I mean, nothing would make me happier than giving you information so you could run to Clay. He could then clue Fernando in. And those two bullies could go over and beat up a little eleven-year-old boy."

"No Naomi," Ernesto protested, "I don't know anything, honest. I was just thinking about something else. I was thinking about running. I've got running in my heart and soul."

"*What*?" Naomi asked, a puzzled look on her face. "Well," Naomi fumed, "if some vicious little boy came over to school and vandalized poor Fernando's car, I think it's a lot more important than thinking about running."

"Connecting with something," Ernesto said. But Naomi had already stomped off. She seemed angry. At this moment, Ernesto didn't like her very much.

When school was over for the day, Ernesto caught up to Carlos Negrete. "Hey man, we need to talk," Ernesto said.

"Go dude," Carlos responded. "I'm all ears."

"Your little brother," Ernesto began, "he was skateboarding yesterday and Fernando Sanchez was roaring down the street like a maniac. He almost hit Estebán and his buddies, and they got furious. Estebán told me he was gonna come over to Chavez and key Fernando's car. And it looks like he did."

Carlos Negrete looked angry. "Good for the kid. That dude is a menace on the road. One of these days he's gonna kill somebody."

"Carlos," Ernesto replied, "I agree with you. But what Estebán did was vandalism, and he could get in big trouble. I know what Fernando does, how he speeds and likes to drive into pigeons, scattering them into the air. He's like a madman. I know all that. But you need to get Estebán to lay low 'cause I wouldn't be surprised if Fernando puts two and two together and comes around to your house to kick his. . . ."

"He touches my little *hermano*, and I'll kill him. I swear I will," Carlos raged.

"Cool it, bro, just cool it," Ernesto advised. "I'm giving you a heads-up so you know what might be coming down."

"Ernie," Carlos said in a low voice, a wild look coming into his eyes. "I bet it was Fernando going down Caldwell Street when Tessie Zamora got hit. I bet he was drunk as a skunk like he often is. He just came speeding down that street and hit that girl. Then he just took off like the rotten coward he is. He got his Honda repaired and painted on the other side of the *barrio*. Meantime, the cops were hunting for a dark green or blue car as the hit-and-run. It all fits, Ernie."

"You could be right," Ernesto admitted, "but how can you prove it now? Probably they cleaned and painted the car so good that there wouldn't be any evidence left."

"You know what, man?" Carlos swore. "I'm gonna talk to Fernando. I'm telling him what I think he did. I'm layin' it on the line.

CHAPTER FOUR

I'm telling him that if he heard any stories about my little brother being the one who keyed his car, he just better forget them. I'm telling him if he makes a move against *mi hermano* I'm goin' to the cops and tell them I think I know who hit Tessie Zamora."

Ernesto took a deep breath. "I don't know, man."

"I'm doin' it, man," Carlos raged. "I'm telling that creep he better not show his face around our house or the school where Estebán goes. I'm not admitting my brother did the keying. I'm just letting the creep know that if he has any ideas to get back at *mi hermano*, he better forget them. Maybe he ducked all those DUI raps, but if he did a hit-and-run that almost killed a girl, he's gonna pay."

Ernesto was sick over the situation. He wondered whether he made a mistake tipping Carlos Negrete off about his brother keying the Honda. But Ernesto was afraid for the boy. Fernando was not the sharpest knife in the drawer. But now that he knew a young boy had done the vandalism, he may just remember the skateboarding incident. He had lived in the *barrio* all his life, and he probably knew Estebán and his friends. Ernesto could imagine Fernando and Clay and a couple of the other football players going to the Negrete neighborhood. They'd catch the boy alone, riding his skateboard like he did every afternoon until almost dark. Ernesto could easily imagine them grabbing the kid and giving him their own brand of vigilante justice.

Ernesto had had to warn Carlos out of fear for the boy. Yet, if Carlos confronted Fernando with the accusation that he was the hit-and-run driver who hurt Tessie, who knew how Fernando would react? A nasty, dangerous fight might break out. Ernesto wondered whether he had opened up a hornet's nest. Maybe now he had no way to control the outcome.

Ernesto tried to get his mind off the problem, but he couldn't. Not even running could ease this problem. The wasps from the hornet's nest were circling, and he wasn't sure who would get stung. The minute Ernesto's father pulled into the driveway that afternoon, Ernesto told him everything.

"Dad, maybe I screwed up, I don't know," Ernesto confided. "I was afraid for Esteban Negrete. Now Carlos is going to confront Fernando and accuse him of that hit-and-run accident with Tessie Zamora. He's gonna tell Fernando that if he makes a move on the boy, then he's gonna expose him to the police as the hit-and-run driver. Dad, I'm afraid something awful might happen and it'd be my fault!"

"Ernesto," Dad replied calmly, "if the Negrete boy keyed that car, then he has to own up to it. It was vandalism, and there's no excuse for that. I know Carlos is your friend, but that doesn't change anything. That doesn't excuse a plan to try to blackmail Fernando into keeping quiet about the hit-and-run accident. Maybe Fernando Sanchez was the driver that day, but we don't know that. Carlos doesn't know that."

"What will we do, Dad?" Ernesto begged desperately.

"Get in the car, *mi hijo*," Dad ordered quietly.

They drove to the Negrete home. Luis Sandoval went into the house alone. When he came out, he told Ernesto that he had convinced Mr. and Mrs. Negrete to stop their son from confronting Fernando Sanchez. "I told them," Dad reported, "tomorrow I will talk to them and try to get the situation straightened out. In the meantime, there must be no confrontation between the boys. They understood. They're fine people. They don't want any trouble."

As Ernesto and his father drove home, Ernesto spoke. "Dad, what if Fernando did drive that hit-and-run car? Do you think he'll get away with this like he's gotten away with everything else?"

"Tomorrow," Dad repeated, "I'll talk to Estebán's parents and try to convince them to make restitution for what their boy did. I believe they will do the right thing. Estebán must learn that, no matter how angry you are at someone, no matter what they have done, you do not take the law into your own hands."

"But what about Fernando. What if he did—" Ernesto started to say.

"I'll contact a police officer I know in the traffic department," Dad responded, "and tell him about the Honda that was repaired and painted out of town shortly after the accident. I think the police will take another look at the car. If it's possible to link it to the crime, then they'll do it."

Ernesto felt better now that his father was involved, but he was still nervous. What if Carlos figured out that he had blown the whistle on Estebán? Carlos and his friends could turn against Ernesto. And if the cops came nosing around Fernando's Honda tomorrow, would he figure Ernesto had something to do with that?

That night, Ernesto didn't sleep well. He had nightmares of different scenarios, all of them bad. He imagined all the kids at Cesar Chavez turning against him. He pictured Carlos and Dom and their friends all lined up waiting for him in the morning.

"Dude," Carlos would say darkly, "you ratted out my brother. What did you do that for? Now my family is stuck paying to have that rat's car fixed. I thought you were my friend, Sandoval, but you're a creep."

Ernesto cringed in his dream. He didn't have a comeback. More and more students— friends of Carlos and Dom—appeared, almost like a mob, wanting to take him down. Ernesto wanted to flee, to get away from the school, but they were right behind him. Even Abel Ruiz turned against him.

And then the football team and all the cheerleaders charged at him. "You tried to frame me for the hit-and-run man," Fernando screamed. "I didn't do it, but you tried to frame me. We ain't gonna kick the football around in practice no more. No, man. We're gonna kick you around!"

Ernesto broke out in a cold sweat. He was wide awake at two in the morning, and he never got back to sleep.

CHAPTER FIVE

Ernesto dreaded going to school in the morning. His father had left very early for his talk with the Negrete family. Ernesto had no idea how that would turn out. Ernesto pushed his eggs and bacon around the plate, unable to get much down. He managed to drink the orange juice, but that was all. By the time Ernesto came to school and saw Carlos and Dom and their friends, Dad would have been to the Negrete house.

As Ernesto parked his Volvo at Cesar Chavez High School, he was tense. When he saw Carlos Negrete coming toward him, he stiffened. He didn't know what to expect. Ernesto stood there, waiting for whatever would happen. Luis Sandoval was a persuasive man, and Ernesto could only hope the meeting this morning had gone well.

"Hey man," Ernesto managed to say from his dry mouth.

"Hey," Carlos replied. "Mr. Sandoval was at my house this morning. Your father came to talk turkey."

"Yeah, I know," Ernesto admitted.

"You told him what *mi hermano* did, dude," Carlos said.

"Yeah, I thought I had to," Ernesto explained. "I was afraid, Carlos, afraid Fernando would find out and come and mix it up with the boy. I figured you and Fernando could get violent and . . ."

Carlos nodded. "My parents, they told your father that they were struggling to raise three boys, three wild boys. They said it wasn't easy, but they were trying. Anyway, your father, he said he knew they were good people and they wanted to do the right thing. Nobody wanted any trouble with the law. So, you know, your dad suggested we offer to help Sanchez get his car fixed. My father said okay. It went pretty well, dude."

"That's a big relief to me," Ernesto responded. "I just wanted everybody to, you know, be okay."

"Your father, he's a good man, dude," Carlos stated slowly. "For a teacher, he ain't half bad. I'm glad he came. I don't blame Estebán for getting ticked off and keying Sanchez's car. I mean, he and his buddies almost got creamed. But still it worried me sick that he'd done it. I figured the little guy might end up in juvie. Estebán goes off half-cocked sometimes. I did too when I was his age. But it's gonna be okay. Estebán has got to do some chores to help pay for the damage."

Carlos paused. "Your old man, I mean your father, he promised to get a friend down at the police station to check out the red Honda. Someone's gonna see if it was the car that hit Tessie. If it was, then Fernando has to face the music, you know.

It's not right that the guy can get away with murder, or what almost was murder."

Carlos stood there with no expression on his face for a few minutes. Then he said with a smile, "Like I said. The dude's okay. He ain't just a teacher, you know. Most of them down there at Chavez, they do their stuff in the classroom, and they go home. But Mr. Sandoval, he's willing to roll up his sleeves and help in other stuff too. That's pretty cool man."

"Yeah," Ernesto agreed.

Ernesto smiled a little too. He and Carlos exchanged fist bumps.

That weekend, Ernesto's grandmother, *Abuela* Lena, moved into the Sandoval home. She had become a widow five years ago when *Abuelo* Luis Sr. died suddenly. Since then, she had lived with *Tía* Magda, her eldest daughter. Everything worked out well there, but recently she had become a little frail. She almost fell once, and Magda was alarmed. Magda and her husband still worked full-time, and they didn't want *Abuela* to be alone in the house all day. Yes, they had an alarm system she could press for help, but still somebody needed to be there. So it was decided she would live with her son and his family.

Everyone in the Sandoval family agreed with the idea of *Abuela* moving in, but the most enthusiastic was six-year-old Juanita. She had a special relationship with *Abuela* that centered around the little girl's large doll house. It had been a Christmas present to her two years ago, and Juanita and eight-year-old Katalina played with it endlessly. But then Katalina developed an interest in other things, like Wii. So Juanita had no-body in the family to play dolls with her. When *Abuela* came to visit, Juanita and her grandmother spent hours arranging and re-arranging the doll house furniture. *Abuela* knitted little bedspreads for the bed and made curtains for the windows. Juanita was always sorry to see the visits end. She would again have nobody in the house who loved the doll house as much as she did. But now that *Abuela* would live with the Sandovals, Juanita looked forward to hours of playing again.

Ernesto's mother was happy to have *Abuela* around too. She was really into writing her book and happy to have her mother-in-law spending time with the girls.

Ernesto's father, of course, loved his mother very much and was glad to know she'd be staying with him and the family. During the ten years they had spent in Los Angeles, he felt bad about having limited contact with her.

Ernesto had always liked *Abuela* more than he liked his mother's Mom because *Abuela* Lena was always cheerful and fun to be with. Eva Vasquez, Mom's mother always seemed a little disappointed when she visited the Sandovals. Ernesto figured their disappointment had to do with Mom never going to college and not fulfilling the great dreams her parents had for her.

CHAPTER FIVE

On Saturday morning, Ernesto drove his Volvo over to Magda's house, followed by Dad in the minivan. They prepared to move *Abuela* from Magda's house to theirs. They had plenty of room in the two cars for a lot of stuff. But they were surprised at how little *Abuela* had. She owned two coats, four sweaters, some dresses, and a few pairs of slacks and pullovers. *Abuela* firmly believed that you should give away whatever you didn't wear on a regular basis. So most of her clothes had been donated. *Abuela*'s personal possessions consisted of a Spanish-language Bible, a rosary, her bankbook, a photo collage with pictures of family, and little else. From one wall, Ernesto took down a large crucifix with a bottle of holy water in a compartment with a sliding cover. From another wall, he took down her picture of Our Lady of Guadalupe. The den at the Sandoval house—the room she was moving into—was already furnished; so she had no furniture to move.

To Ernesto went the honor of bringing *Abuela* home in his Volvo.

"What a nice, roomy car, Ernesto," *Abuela* noted as they pulled out of the driveway. She usually called him Ernesto instead of Ernie, as almost everyone else did. Just as she always called her husband Lucho. She smiled as she sat beside her grandson and declared, "I am so proud of you, Ernesto. Most boys and girls your age want a sporty kind of car. But you chose a nice, sensible, safe car."

"Don't I know it!" Ernesto laughed. "The kids at school really gave me a hard time when I pulled up in this. But this is the only reliable car I could afford. Later on I'll get a car I like better."

"I hope I won't be making problems for your family, Ernesto," *Abuela* Lena confided with a suddenly serious look on her face. "It is sometimes difficult when an older person moves in."

Ernesto glanced and smiled at his grandmother. "We're all happy you're moving in, *Abuela*. I just hope my sisters don't wear you out, especially Juanita with that doll house! I think that girl is going to be an interior decorator when she grows up. She's moving stuff around all the time."

"Remember now, Ernesto," *Abuela* advised, "when you have your young friends over, I won't mind at all how much noise they make. I love to hear children having a good time. You can play your music as loud as you want. I do not even mind the rock and roll and the rap. The neighbors at Magda's house had young people. They had a little rock band, and it was very loud. But I liked it because they were so happy when they beat on their drums."

"Yeah," Ernesto recollected, "I remember when we still lived here in the *barrio*. You and *Abuelo* would let *Tía* Hortencia make a big racket with her friends. I was really small then, but your house seemed to shake with the music."

Abuela smiled, but a shadow of sadness fell over her eyes. "I miss your grandfather.

Those were lovely days. But, like it says in the *Biblia*, there is a time to laugh and a time to cry. But we will try to laugh as much as possible, eh Ernesto?"

"Yeah," Ernesto agreed. "You bet." Ernesto wondered whether his grandmother knew the Martinez family very well when Felix and his wife Linda were youngsters. He wondered what she thought of them, but he didn't want to ask.

"Ernesto, you are so handsome," *Abuela* commented. "Do you have a girlfriend? Or do you have many?"

Ernesto shrugged. "There's a girl I like, *Abuela*. But she's not so much interested in me."

"Ah, that may change," Ernesto's grandmother advised as they pulled up to the house. "When you are young, your emotions are like the wind. Every day they change."

Ernesto and his father took all *Abuela*'s possessions into the house. Her few clothes didn't come close to filling the big closet.

She was delighted by the bedspread with the geraniums on it and by the view from the window of the birdbath. Ernesto hung her crucifix and her picture of Our Lady of Guadalupe where she wanted them. Then he hung her collage of photographs: her wedding picture with a handsome *Abuelo*, her five children and their spouses, and her grandchildren. In one of the photographs, Ernesto found himself standing solemnly between his parents when he was four.

"Mama!" came a joyful shout as Hortencia came bursting into the house. She grabbed her mother and hugged her. "Oh, I am so happy you are here! It's much closer for me to come visit." They sat down and began speaking excitedly in Spanish. Ernesto had to grin at their topic of conversation. (He spoke Spanish fluently.) He heard his grandmother ask her unmarried daughter whether there was a young man on the horizon. After all, *Abuela* pointed out, Hortencia was already in her thirties and she needed to seriously think of settling down. *Tía* Hortencia just giggled and told her mother that she was dating a wonderful musician now and that things looked quite promising.

Later that afternoon, Ernesto drove over to the pizzeria to pick up his paycheck. During that drive, he noticed Fernando's red Honda coming up behind him. In the rearview mirror, Ernesto saw the Honda swerve into the oncoming lane, then pass the Volvo illegally. Fernando was driving too fast as usual.

Fernando's girlfriend, Rosalie Rivas, was with him in the car. Naomi and Rosalie were quite close. All the cheerleaders were. That was why Tessie's accident was such a blow to them. Rosalie was one of the few Mexican girls with blonde hair. She told Naomi that her family came from a part of Mexico where many of the people were blonde. But Ernesto thought she probably dyed her hair. Rosalie was the second prettiest girl on the cheerleading squad—after Naomi. Ernesto had seen Fernando with

Rosalie quite a lot recently. They walked hand in hand at school, and sometimes they sneaked behind the science building and kissed. Ernesto did not like Fernando, but he surely treated Rosalie a lot better than Clay Aguirre treated Naomi. Ernesto wondered why Naomi didn't notice that difference in attitude. Fernando never called Rosalie "stupid," like Clay called Naomi, even though Rosalie was not very smart and Naomi had almost straight As in school.

A homecoming party was planned for Tessie Zamora the coming Friday evening. Her parents were bringing her home from the hospital, and all her friends wanted to decorate her room as a surprise. Tessie loved pandas. So everybody chipped in to buy her a panda bedspread, and on her dressing table waited a cute stuffed panda.

Tessie had been impressed with Ernesto when he brought Naomi to the hospital to visit her. She made a special request that he come to her homecoming party. Ernesto didn't mind going, but the thought that Clay Aguirre would be there with Naomi disgusted him. All the cheerleaders were coming with their boyfriends. Despite Tessie's special request, Carmen Ibarra offered to come with Ernesto so he wouldn't be the only guy there without a girl.

That Friday, Ernesto and Carmen went over to the Zamoras' house early to help decorate. They hung balloons and party streamers around a large "Welcome Home, Tessie!" sign.

"We're so happy to have her home," Tessie's mother told Ernesto and Carmen. "We've been through such torment since this happened. We thought for days after the accident that we were going to lose her. Here we were, my husband and I worrying about our son in the Middle East, and our baby girl nearly got killed a few blocks from our house!"

"Yeah, that was a terrible accident," Ernesto affirmed.

"When we visited Tessie, she talked about you, Ernie," Mrs. Zamora told him, glancing at Carmen to see whether her comment had any effect on her. "She said Naomi brought such a nice and handsome boy with her. She said you even gave her a kiss and a hug. That made her feel better than all the physical therapy and the medicine. Ernie, I think Tessie has a crush on you!" The small dark woman laughed.

Ernesto felt his skin turn warm. "She's a beautiful and courageous girl," he replied. "To have gone through so much and to keep her spirits up."

Ernesto and Carmen finished hanging the balloons, and they got ready to go. They would return in a couple hours for the party.

Before they left, Mr. Zamora approached them and spoke. "Tessie has a long road ahead of her." He was a short, nervous-looking man. "She will have to use crutches for some time. Then there will be a lot of physical therapy. But we are so grateful to God that she was not taken from us. Our little girl survived. It was a hit-and-run you know, Ernesto." The man's face turned sad and angry.

"Yeah, I know," Ernesto affirmed. "I can't imagine anybody doing that."

Mr. Zamora did not look as though he was capable of violence. But now he declared in a grim voice, "If I ever meet the *hombre* who hit my child and left her to die in the street, I will kill him with my own two bare hands." Ernesto didn't say anything. He hurried out with Carmen.

Two hours later, they returned for the party. The Zamoras would soon pull up with Tessie, and they would take her up the walk in a wheelchair. Everybody was told to come at least fifteen minutes early so that they could all shout their welcome with one voice as Tessie came in.

By the time Ernesto and Carmen had arrived, Clay Aguirre was already there with Naomi. Fernando was with Rosalie, and the other cheerleaders and their boyfriends were arriving. Ernesto glanced quickly at

Fernando. The possibility that he was the person who hit Tessie and fled gave Ernesto a creepy feeling. Here he was laughing and acting as if nothing was wrong. Rosalie looked very tense, though. She had been at the hospital almost every day sitting with Tessie. The accident really seemed to have hit her hard.

When the Zamoras pushed Tessie's wheelchair through the front door, everybody yelled and clapped. Tessie saw the huge banner, signed by dozens of her friends, saying, "Welcome Home, Tessie!"

"Oh my gosh! You guys!" Tessie cried, tears running down her cheeks. "You guys!"

Rosalie Rivas rushed to the wheelchair to hug Tessie first, and everybody else followed. Rosalie seemed to hover near the wheelchair, not wanting to be separated from her friend. Ernesto wondered whether Fernando *was* the hit-and-run driver and maybe Rosalie knew or suspected that he was. That would explain why Rosalie seemed so emotional. But, if she did know for sure or even suspect him, Ernesto couldn't imagine how Rosalie could stay with Fernando.

As the partygoers drifted away from the wheelchair, Tessie's gaze swept across all the faces in the room, settling on Ernesto's. "Oh! You *did* come!" she cried out happily. "I was afraid you wouldn't!"

"Hey!" Ernesto called out, stepping toward her. "I wouldn't have missed it. You look great, Tessie. I bet you'll be back at Chavez in no time. We got all wheelchair-accessible ramps and stuff. You'll do fine."

"Yeah," Tessie declared, "I want to go back as soon as I can. I'm just so anxious to have my life back again. It's been so lonely. Rosie and the rest of you guys have been wonderful coming to see me. But I hated being stuck in that hospital. I just missed *everything*!"

"You know what, Tessie?" Naomi announced. "You can be part of the cheerleading squad again right away. You can wave the pom-poms and yell. You can come to all the games and stuff."

"Oh that'd be so fun," Tessie said. "I miss all you guys so much. I even miss the teachers. Can you believe that?"

"You should've been at the game last week," Clay Aguirre interrupted. "Naomi goofed up the routine really bad. She almost fell down and took Rosalie down with her! I've never seen such clumsy cheerleaders in my life. It was hilarious. I mean, we football players stumble around, but cheerleaders are supposed to be graceful." Clay laughed long and loud over his account of the incident.

Naomi looked hurt. "It wasn't that bad, Clay," she said in a quiet little voice. "I just slipped on some dirt and lost my balance for a second."

"You saw it, Nando," Clay crowed, still laughing. "Wasn't it wild?" Fernando laughed too.

Naomi walked away to join the other girls in putting out the cookies and cupcakes. Two boys brought some *horchata* and *agua fresca*. Naomi looked unhappy, still smarting over Clay's remark. But Ernesto was sort of glad Clay made his remarks. Maybe if Clay did enough stuff like that, Naomi would wake up and see him for the rude jerk he was.

Rosalie and the other girls put a cupcake and some cookies on each paper plate. She brought Tessie's to her with a glass of *agua fresca*. Ernesto continued to wonder why Rosalie was so helpful to Tessie— more so than anybody else. Maybe, he thought, they had been best friends for a long time.

"Mmm! Thanks Rose," Tessie cooed. "Chocolate cupcakes, my favorite. And look at those cookies. They're so good. You guys are just amazing. I'm so grateful to have nice friends like you. I was feeling sorry for myself in the hospital, but I'm actually lucky. How many girls have the kind of friends I have?"

"That's because you're so lovable, Tessie," Carmen told her. "You're the best."

"Ernie," Tessie requested, "come over here and sit by me. I know everybody else, but you're a stranger to me. I gotta know all about you. You said you were born around here and you guys just moved down from Los Angeles. You got brothers and sisters?"

"I have two little sisters, Katalina and Juanita," Ernesto answered. "They're much younger than me. And my mom is gonna have another baby too. So I'll have a little brother or sister who's like seventeen years younger than me."

"Oh, that's cool," Tessie replied. "I'd love to have little brothers and sisters. I got just one brother, and he's overseas fighting in the war. I worry about him a lot. I'm hoping when he gets home, he'll marry his girlfriend and they'll have kids. Then I'll have some little kids to spoil and buy toys for. Ernie, your dad is a teacher at Chavez, huh?"

Naomi chimed in. "Tessie, he's the best. He's just one of those teachers that don't come around too often. When you meet one, you feel so lucky. I have him in American history, and I just look forward so much to that class."

Ernesto felt a rush of gratitude to Naomi.

"Ernie," Tessie asked, "that promise to take me for a chicken *enchilada* still stands, right?"

"You bet," Ernesto said, grinning.

CHAPTER SIX

He's kind of a wimp, Tessie," Clay Aguirre chimed in. "Old Ernie here, he drives a Volvo, a granny car. You sure you wanna be seen in a granny car?"

Ernesto didn't want to start anything. So he ignored Clay's bait. He didn't want to get into a yelling match with the creep just when poor Tessie got home from the hospital.

"Wow!" Tessie declared. "I'd ride with a guy that cute in a hotdog wagon. Ernie is hot!"

Ernesto didn't know about being hot. He didn't feel as though he was, but he was touched that Tessie would say so. All of a sudden Ernesto was aware of Naomi staring at him. "Ernie, you've been working out, haven't you?" she inquired. "I thought I noticed something different about you."

"Yeah," Ernesto admitted. "I'm doing a little weight lifting, stuff like that. I'm running and doing push-ups, just trying to build my strength, you know."

"Your chest looks bigger," Naomi commented. "You really look great, Ernie. You look ripped."

A dark look crossed Clay Aguirre's face. He didn't like Naomi noticing that any other guy looked ripped. He didn't like it one bit. Clay was infuriated that Naomi had complimented Ernesto.

"You using steroids, Sandoval?" Clay asked in a nasty voice. "You look like maybe that's what you're doing."

"No, I don't get into that kind of stuff," Ernesto replied. "It's a really bad idea, I think."

"You're a regular Goody Two-shoes, aren't you, Sandoval?" Clay snarled sharply. "I bet you read bedtime stories to your kid sisters. And I hear your granny just moved in, so maybe you and her knit doilies together."

"Sure," Ernesto agreed with a sly smile. "My favorite story is about the three bears." Everybody laughed, and Clay looked even angrier.

"You're on the track team, right, Ernie?" Tessie asked. "I love to watch runners. When the Olympics are on TV, I always watch the track events. I think they're so thrilling. Runners, they're really the most amazing athletes because they don't depend on a team. They're like running against their own personal best, and that is so cool. Track is really the biggest test of an athlete."

"Yeah!" Carmen, who had been unusually quiet, chimed in. She resented how Clay was baiting Ernesto, and she decided to give him some of his own medicine. "In football so much depends on all the guys working together. You can throw a great pass, but when somebody fumbles it, the whole team suffers." Carmen meant that as a put-down.

When Ernesto had realized that Clay Aguirre would be at this party, he almost didn't come. But he had promised Tessie, and he hadn't wanted to disappoint her. But now he felt nervous. Guys like Clay had a way of turning parties into disasters. So Ernesto tried to change the subject.

"Did you guys hear about the mural Dom and Carlos are making on the side of the science building?" he asked everyone at large. "About a dozen kids'll be working on it. It's gonna be really great. The TV station is gonna come out and do a feature on it when it's finished. It's gonna show Cesar Chavez leading that grape strike. It should really spruce up the school."

"Yeah, that'll be cool," Tessie agreed.

They started talking about Cesar Chavez and how he worked for the poor more than forty years ago. That was at a time when their own parents were little kids or not even born.

"We should remember people like him," Tessie advised, "'cause they made life better for a lot of people."

The change of subject worked. Clay was quiet for the rest of the party, which broke up around nine. Ernesto was never so glad to get away from anything as he was to flee the presence of Clay Aguirre. Fernando wasn't causing any trouble. But he seemed oddly on edge, and Rosalie looked weird.

"Man!" Ernesto exclaimed as he and Carmen walked to his Volvo. "Remind me never again to go to anything where Aguirre is likely to show up."

Carmen laughed. "I hear you," she chuckled. "That's why Pop won't let him come to our house. He came one time and started fights with two other guys. He's just so ugly."

At the car, Ernesto opened the car door for Carmen, closed it, and then came around to the driver's side. He noticed Clay and Naomi leaving too. They were heading for Clay's Mustang.

"What'd you want to make a fool of me like that for?" Clay was yelling at Naomi.

"Oh brother!" Ernesto muttered to Carmen as he slid behind the wheel. "Look at the jerk making a show of himself . . . "

Naomi and Clay started arguing loudly. "I don't know what you're talking about," Naomi snapped back. "Calm down, Clay."

"Don't be any stupider than you already are, babe," Clay yelled. "You had to be drooling over that creep Sandoval. You just went on and on about his big muscles and how ripped he was. What was that all about, girl? How do you think that made me feel?" He was yelling so loudly that everyone leaving the party could hear him.

"Clay," Naomi came back angrily. "You were making fun of me messing up the cheer routine at the game. That wasn't very nice. I didn't get all bent out of shape over that. So just cool it, will you?"

"Oh, is that why you were making over Sandoval?" Clay snarled. "To get even for me saying how you ruined the cheerleading routine?"

"Clay, can we just get out of here?" Naomi insisted in a cross voice.

But Clay Aguirre wasn't finished. "You got the hots for Sandoval, don't you? I'm not blind. I see what's right before my eyes!" Clay was standing in front of Naomi, towering over her, yelling in her face.

"Clay, are you crazy?" Naomi cried. "You know how I feel about you!"

Clay pushed her against the side of the car, pinning her there, yelling in her face. "You made a fool of me in front of everybody! I'm here to tell you, babe, I don't like that one bit. I don't take stuff like that from no chick!"

Ernesto shoved open his car door and jumped out, heading for Clay.

"Be careful," Carmen yelled. "He's bigger than you!"

Ernesto sprinted toward the Mustang as Clay was poking his finger into Naomi's face. He stopped a couple of steps short. He was close enough to see that Naomi looked startled. Her feelings were hurt when Clay humiliated her by recalling the cheerleading snafu. And yes, she was looking for a little revenge by complimenting Ernesto. But she never thought it would come to this. Now she looked frightened.

"Knock it off, man," Ernesto commanded. "Knock it off right now."

"It's okay, Ernie," she said hastily. "We're fine. We're just having a little argument."

"You skinny little freak," Clay raged, turning on Ernesto. "Who do you think you are? You come marching up here, sticking your nose into somebody else's business!"

Ernesto wasn't sure what was going to happen next. If Clay charged Ernesto, he could do serious damage. Ernesto knew that, but he had to intervene. Clay had looked as though he was about to slap Naomi. Ernesto couldn't just stand by and let that happen. Ernesto acted on instinct, and it was too late to backpedal now.

"Hey, what's all the yelling about?" Fernando Sanchez shouted as he and Rosalie came out of the Zamora house.

"Me and Naomi were talking, and this fool comes over and tries to start something," Clay claims.

Fernando looked at Ernesto and advised, "Don't try to take on a football player, dude. Guys like us towel off with twerps like you."

Then he turned to Clay. "Dude, keep it down. They were hearing you and Naomi screaming at each other in the house, and the old folks got upset, you know? If you got a problem with your chick, take it home. Don't settle it on the street."

Mr. Zamora turned on the porch light and called out, "Is everything all right out there?"

"Yeah!" Fernando called back. "It's all cool."

Rosalie looked at Naomi. "You want a ride home with us?" she asked.

"No," Naomi declined. "Everything's fine. Just fine. This is a big deal over nothing."

Ernesto looked at Naomi. For just a second their gazes clicked together. Naomi knew she was seconds away from getting a nasty slap across her face when Ernesto intervened. She knew it and Ernesto knew it.

In that second, Naomi felt regret and shame. She blamed herself, not Clay. She never should have given Ernesto such a compliment in front of Clay. She knew what buttons not to push when she was with Clay. She had ignored her better sense. She knew well enough the things that would drive Clay into frenzied anger, and she always stayed clear of them. Naomi berated herself. "This whole thing is my fault," she thought, flooded with misery. She had made Clay look bad.

Naomi resolved never to make such a mistake again. She would never push Clay's buttons like that again. Naomi felt terrible that Ernesto had seen Clay at his worst. The awful part was that she could have avoided all of it. Naomi knew what to say and what not to say when she was with Clay. Why had she allowed her irritation over that silly cheerleading incident drive her to anger him so much? She let her stupid pride get the better of her.

Naomi quickly got into the Mustang and pulled the door shut. Clay came around the driver's side and got behind the wheel. When he took off, he left a lot of rubber in the street.

Fernando laughed. "Like a bat out of hell," he crowed.

Ernesto felt sick at the core of his soul.

Rosalie had a sad look on her face, but she snuggled close to Fernando. "Tessie is gonna be okay, isn't she?" she asked hopefully. "I bet she's good as new in no time, huh?"

Fernando slipped his arm around the girl's shoulders. "Yeah baby, next year this time, her accident is gonna be just a bad memory."

"Yeah," Rosalie echoed. Fernando leaned over and kissed her. Then they walked to their car.

Ernesto overheard their conversation. He didn't know what to make of Rosalie's concern. Then he wheeled and went back to the car.

"Well," Carmen declared as he got behind the wheel, "all I can say is, thank God Tessie never saw what happened out here. What a creep that Clay is!"

"It was a nice party except for him," Ernesto remarked.

"I've got to make a note of it," Carmen announced. "When I get married, Naomi will not be one of the bridesmaids if she's still with Clay. I mean, me and Naomi been friends since first grade. I'd love for her to be in my wedding when it happens. But if she's still with him . . . "

Carmen shook her head and fell silent for a few seconds while Ernesto pulled away from the curb. Then she changed the subject. "Your grandma all moved in, Ernie?"

"Yeah," he replied, glad to switch to a happier subject. "I couldn't believe how little stuff she had. Seventy-five years old, and all she's got is like a fourth of the closet, some photos, her religious stuff. Man, she travels light."

"Everything working out?" Carmen asked.

"Yeah!" Ernesto shook his head yes. "Mom is real excited about her book. Katalina gave Mom this idea about a nice pit bull making friends with a cat, and she's going with that. She contacted this pit bull rescue association, and they sent her all kinds of good stuff about the breed. It seems some pit pulls are therapy dogs in nursing homes and hospitals. Can you beat that? Mom's glad that *Abuela* is spending time with the girls. Frees her time up for the book."

When Carmen didn't respond right away, Ernesto noticed that she'd been unusually quiet. "Carmen, how come you're not talking so much? You're not sick or something are you?"

Carmen gave a short little laugh. "No!" she chuckled.

"What's the matter then?" Ernesto asked.

"I'm kinda worried about Rosie," Carmen admitted. "Did you see how she was crying at the party?"

"Yeah, I just thought she was happy that Tessie is doing so good. You know, tears of joy," Ernesto suggested. "I don't know Rosalie Rivas that well. I can't say if she normally cries a lot."

"She never used to cry," Carmen attested. "She was always happy-go-lucky, Ernie. In all the time I've known her, I've seen her cry only a couple times. Now she cries a lot."

"She and Fernando seem to get along good," Ernesto noted. "He's always hugging her. He's not putting her down like Clay is with Naomi."

"Yeah, they get along good," Carmen agreed. "Fernando is kinda creepy. He drinks, and sometimes he drinks and drives.

I hate that. But he's nice to Rosie. He always has been."

"Is there maybe trouble in her family?" Ernesto asked. "Every family has problems. Maybe some dark secret is bothering her, like her parents not getting along."

"I don't think so, Ernie," Carmen objected. "Rosie just seems depressed. I haven't seen her laugh in moons."

"Maybe she should go see a doctor," Ernesto suggested. "You see these ads on TV about people getting real sad for no reason. Then they go to a doctor, and there's help out there, I guess."

"I think I'll talk to her, Ernie," Carmen said. "I'll tell her to see a doctor if she can't shake the blues."

Ernesto pulled into the Ibarras' driveway. "Thanks for coming with me, Carmen," Ernesto told her as he put on the parking brake. "It made me feel a lot better to have a girl with me."

Carmen smiled. "My pleasure, Ernie!" Then she turned her head toward the house.

"Did you just see the curtain move in the front window? That's Papa. He thinks we're into each other. He wants to make sure there's no funny business going on. But he likes you, Ernie. He really likes you."

Ernesto put on a mock frightened look. "I'm glad he does! He's a nice guy." He was still a little bit afraid of Emilio Zapata Ibarra. Ernesto then walked Carmen to the door to see her safely inside.

"I do too," Carmen added as they stepped up on the porch.

"You do too what?" Ernesto asked her.

"Like you," she confessed.

"Oh," Ernesto said. "I like you too, Carmen."

"You could at least give me a little peck!" Carmen was flirting with him.

Ernesto gently grasped the girl's shoulders and kissed her on the forehead.

"Doesn't count!" Carmen protested.

Ernesto cradled Carmen's face in his hands and kissed her gently on the lips.

"Tessie's right," Carmen sighed breathlessly.

"Huh?" Ernesto said.

"You're hot," Carmen told him, hurrying inside—just as her father scampered away from the window, grinning from ear to ear.

When Ernesto got home, Mom was still on the computer.

"How's it going, Mom?" he asked her.

"Really good!" she said. "You know, on the surface, this is a story about pit bulls, but it's much more than that. It's about something deeper, honey." Mom sounded really charged up. It was fun to see her so excited about something that was all hers. She was always jazzed about Dad's successes and the children doing well in school, but now she had her own thing.

"It's about not judging a book by its cover." Mrs. Sandoval was pushed back from the computer a little and musing. "Ernie, we see a pit bull, and we think 'Ooooo, mean, bad dog.' But we look at people like that too. We see a different skin color, a different shape of eyes, hair that isn't like ours, and we judge those people. Maybe they have a different way of worshipping, or they speak with an accent. We can't see their hearts. We shouldn't judge anybody on external things. That's what the book is really about."

"That sounds terrific, Mom," Ernesto responded.

"I'm getting a lot of work done it too. *Abuela* has given me a lot of free time. Last night, she read the girls a story," Mom went on. "I used to do that, but then I thought they were getting too old for bedtime stories. Oh boy, was I wrong! Katalina is a good reader, and Juanita is reading a lot too. But, oh, did they enjoy somebody reading to them. You know something, Ernie? *Abuela* liked living with Magda, but she told me it's more fun at our house."

Mom giggled. "Did Tessie enjoy her homecoming party?"

"Oh yeah," Ernesto replied. "She was thrilled with all her friends being there and stuff. She's so glad to be home, Mom. Tessie's really popular. She misses all the stuff she's involved in."

"Terrible thing that happened to her," Mom commented. "I remember her when she was a little girl. Other kids came around on Halloween wanting candy, and she was collecting for the poor. She's always had such a big heart, even then. Makes me sick to think someone—maybe someone we know—struck her and left her lying in the street."

"Dad talked to his friend down at the police station," Ernesto told her. "They're checking out that red Honda that Fernando Sanchez drives. Right after the accident, you know, he took it somewhere out of town and got it repaired and painted. Probably it had nothing to do with Tessie's accident. But Fernando does drive after he's been drinking, and . . ." Ernesto shook his head.

"I almost hope," Mom asserted, "that it wasn't Fernando or anybody else we know, Ernie. I know it would be good to have the crime solved, but it would be so much worse if the Sanchez boy was responsible. He has his faults, but I can't see him hitting Tessie and then just driving away. I know his parents, and they tend to be too easy on Fernando. But they're good people, and a hit-and-run is just so over the top in bad behavior."

Ernesto's father heard the conversation from the kitchen and came out to the living room. "I don't think they can retrieve evidence anymore from the car," he said. "It was thoroughly cleaned and painted. Ernie, I could be very wrong. But Fernando is in my American history class, and I just don't think he's the hit-and-run driver. He's got a lot of faults. He's far from perfect, but I just don't think he did it."

"Yeah," Ernesto agreed. "There're a lot of dark Hondas around. Coulda been somebody who didn't even see Tessie, I guess . . .

somebody from across town. Coulda been an elderly driver who hit her and didn't even know it. I mean, up in LA there was a kid in my class who hit a deer when he was driving in the mountains. He didn't even know he'd done it. He thought he'd hit a deep rut in the road. He pulled over and only then saw the dead deer. His car was damaged, but he was shocked to see he'd killed this big deer."

CHAPTER SEVEN

Ernesto took a shower and headed for bed. Many possibilities raced through his mind. As Mom said, it was hard to know what people were really like—what was in their hearts. It was even hard sometimes to know yourself. Could the person who drove the car that hit Tessie Zamora be a good person, a person as good as, say, Ernesto Sandoval? Could the driver have been so paralyzed by fear that he or she went a little crazy and just fled?

Ernesto lay on his bed, wide awake, thinking. The curtain was open a slit, and the moonlight spilled a white beam across his blanket. What had happened tonight at Tessie's party unnerved him more than he realized. He always knew that Clay Aguirre was rude to Naomi. He called her names. But until tonight, Ernesto never thought Clay was capable of striking her. Yet there in the darkness outside the Zamora house, Clay was full of dark rage. He had pushed Naomi against the car, and he seemed on the verge of hitting her. Ernesto felt in his gut that Clay would have done it.

People did terrible things, Ernesto thought. He remembered Yvette, who'd dropped her abusive boyfriend and begun dating a nice guy, Tommy Alvarado. The old boyfriend tracked them down and killed Tommy. Maybe before the guy killed Tommy, he had abused Yvette. Maybe the warning signs were there, and nobody wanted to see them.

Eventually, Ernesto fell asleep, but nightmares soon overtook him. He dreamed he found Clay beating Naomi. He dreamed she was cowering on the ground, her face bruised and discolored. Ernesto saw a two-by-four lying nearby, and he picked it up.

125

He hit Clay with it again and again until he lay the ground, very still. Ernesto didn't know whether Clay was dead or not, but he was bloody and he didn't move. All Ernesto knew was that this time Clay had gone too far. Something had to be done to stop him. Clay had hurt Naomi.

Ernesto dreamed that he walked over to where Naomi cowered on the ground. He took her hands and raised her up. He said, "He won't ever hurt you anymore."

But Naomi pulled free of Ernesto's hands, and she ran to where Clay Aguirre lay. She took him in her arms and held him, rocking him back and forth as if she were trying to wake him up. But she couldn't. She finally looked up at Ernesto with her bruised and discolored face. She said in a withering voice, "I loved him. I loved him more than life itself. Look at what you did, Ernesto Sandoval. I hate you. I will hate you to my dying day. Clay wasn't bad. He was never bad. I just made him so mad this time that he beat me without knowing what he was doing. He lost it. Now look what you did. I loved him . . . I loved him."

Ernesto woke up with a start. It was one in the morning. He was perspiring. The nightmare was the worst he had ever had. It was a mixture of what happened at Tessie's party and the thought of Tessie lying wounded in the street that day. All the images jumbled together in Ernesto's mind.

Something new had happened tonight, out there in the dark street by the Zamora house. A fear entered Ernesto's mind and heart that had not been there. He cared about Naomi, and it hurt to see Clay being rude to her. But he never before thought Clay might actually hurt the girl. Now Ernesto thought he might.

Ernesto couldn't sleep any longer. He got out of bed, went into the kitchen, and poured himself a glass of milk. He heard somewhere that milk might help you sleep.

"*Abuela*!" Ernesto gasped when his grandmother came into the kitchen. "Can't you sleep either?"

"I have terrible insomnia, Ernesto," she explained. "When I can't sleep, I read recipe books. I was thinking about making something special tomorrow. You know, your mama sent her book proposal to the agent, and she's expecting a call tomorrow. If it's good news, we must celebrate. If the agent likes the proposal, your mama can finish the book and this is happy news. I could make something extra special for the happy occasion. I love to cook."

Abuela did not look seventy-five years old. She had smooth skin and lively black eyes. Certain expressions on her face made her look much younger, like now. She was excited about her daughter-in-law's book. She looked ten or fifteen years younger.

"*Muchacho*," *Abuela* asked, "what has spoiled your night's sleep? You're sitting here in the middle of the night drinking milk with an old lady instead of sleeping."

Ernesto smiled. "I had a horrible nightmare. When I was a little boy, I sometimes got nightmares, and I'd run to my parents room. They'd console me and assure me there weren't any monsters under my bed. But now I am having nightmares about real things that might happen. That's worse."

"Maybe it was something you ate," *Abuela* suggested.

"No," Ernesto started to explain, as *Abuela* sat down at the table with him, her cookbook closed in front of her. "There's this girl I really like at school, Naomi Martinez. She's got this big ugly boyfriend who's all the time yelling at her and putting her down. Tonight we were all at a party, and he looked like he was gonna take a swing at her. I figured he was gonna slap her across the face, and I sort of intervened. I think Naomi was more mad at me than she was at him. That's what gave me the nightmare. Right before I fell asleep I was thinking about what had happened."

"I know Naomi Martinez," *Abuela* replied. "I remember when she was born. They had all boys, and then she came. Her mother was so happy she finally had a girl."

"You know *Abuela*," Ernesto continued, "at school it looks like Naomi and Clay—the boyfriend—are just a happy couple. But there's a darkness in him. He doesn't treat her right and it makes me sick."

Abuela shook her head. "Dark secrets," she remarked.

"What?" Ernesto asked.

"Every family has them, *muchacho*, but some are darker than others," *Abuela* advised.

"Naomi's father," Ernesto said, "Felix Martinez, he's kinda mean to Naomi's mother."

"Mean streaks run in some families like a bloody thread, causing pain," the old woman noted.

"Mom wants me to just forget about Naomi," Ernesto told his grandmother, "'cause if she puts up with a guy like Clay Aguirre, then she can't be worth much. But I can't forget about her. I like her a lot. I feel sorry for her. When I think she might be hurt, I get angry and frustrated."

Abuela opened her cookbook and leafed through it for a few minutes. Ernesto didn't think she was interested in the recipes. Then she looked up at her grandson and spoke.

"Linda Martinez, the girl's mother," grandmother explained, "she came from a family where there was abuse. Nobody knew. The neighbors didn't even know. In those days everything was kept secret. It wasn't like now where women can go to safe houses. There were loud voices and crying, but people believed you should mind your own business. Poor Linda. As a child, she got used to that. When she met Felix Martinez, she did not expect anything different. She didn't get anything different either. Linda has had a difficult life."

"I'm not gonna abandon Naomi," Ernesto declared emotionally. "I'm gonna be there for her if she needs me. I'm not gonna push myself on her or anything, but I'm gonna be her friend. I mean, maybe she doesn't see me in the same way I see her.

Maybe she never will, and that's okay. I can take it. But I'm gonna be there for her if she needs me."

Ernesto's grandmother smiled. "You are your father's son, Ernesto. That's something your father would have said about a friend in trouble when he was your age."

The next day was Saturday, and Maria Sandoval was expecting the important call from her agent. She had sent in her outline, the proposal for the book, and her research on pit bulls. Mom wasn't an artist. So, if the book was taken on, the publisher would hire an artist to do the illustrations. But Mom's name would be on the book cover.

As Mom went about making the Saturday morning breakfast, she giggled, looking as though she were eighteen instead of in her late thirties. "Imagine," she exclaimed, "Maria Sandoval in bold print on the cover of a book! Imagine my mom's reaction. She has about given up that anything I do will be as dramatic and important as she and Papa dreamed for me.

Oh, if something I've written would be published, Mom would run all over the neighborhood showing it to her friends. She would drive everybody crazy bragging about it." Mom giggled again. "But I'm not counting on anything just yet. Thousands of people have written books and are trying to get them published."

"The agent is going to say yes, Mama," Katalina declared firmly. "She'll want your book. She'll sell it to a publisher, and you'll be famous. I know it Mama, because it's a wonderful book. Besides, I gave you the idea."

Dad laughed. "Oh Katalina, it must be a wonderful book if you gave Mama the idea. You have a wonderful imagination."

"I'm going to write books too when I grow up," Katalina announced. "My teacher says I write nice stories, and I write better than most kids my age."

The phone rang early that morning. Ernesto was grateful for that. Everybody was on edge waiting for the other shoe to drop. Mom rushed to answer the phone, saying ruefully, "I bet it's some guy selling insurance!"

But it wasn't an insurance salesperson. It was Janet Wilmington, Mom's would-be agent. *Abuela*, Dad, Ernesto, and the girls all watched Mom's face, watching for clues.

"Yes Janet, I understand," Mom spoke into the phone.

Ernesto's heart sank. It sounded like bad news. He had expected that. Like his father, Ernesto tended to expect bad news. It was an old family trait. Mom did not look happy. The agent did not want to represent her book, Ernesto concluded. Mom was a thirty-seven-year-old housewife with no writing experience. She wasn't a teacher or anything. How could she have written a book worth publishing?

Dad looked crestfallen too. His eyes filled with concern as he plotted ways to console and cheer Mom when she hung up the phone.

"Of course, of course, I expected that, Janet," Mom said. "It's the first children's book I've written."

Ernesto and his father exchanged sad and concerned looks. The agent was telling Mom that she couldn't expect an agent to represent a brand-new author's first book.

"Oh absolutely," Mom agreed. "I don't have a problem with that at all." Mom was putting on a brave front. That was so like her. Her dreams had just been crushed, but she was okay. Her rising star had fallen from the sky, but she would make the best of things. "Oh yes, yes, Janet. Thank you so much. I'll get on it right away."

Mom hung up and turned to her family. Dad, Ernesto, and the girls all seemed to lean forward slightly, bracing themselves against the bad news.

"She wants a revision, some changes, but . . .

"But?" everyone in her family echoed the word mentally.

"But she's going to represent me, you guys," Mom beamed. "She loves the book! Janet Wilmington, who has been the agent for so many successful books, is going to represent me! She's sure she can sell it!"

Luis Sandoval bounded across the room, swept his wife off her feet, and twirled her in a circle. He hugged her and kissed her. They danced around the living room, almost knocking over the floor lamp. Then Ernesto and *Abuela* and the girls all hugged Maria Sandoval in a big group.

"Mama! Mama!" Ernesto's mother said to her mother-in-law, "you brought me good luck. I was able to finish the proposal because you were with the girls so much! *Gracias!*"

"*Por nada*," *Abuela* laughed. "It was a joy for me."

"Oh Mama!" Katalina bubbled over. "You'll be famous. You'll be like the lady who wrote about Harry Potter."

"Oh come on," Mom protested. "Let's not go overboard. Janet has agreed to represent me, but the book is not sold yet to a publisher. And hardly any books are as successful as Harry Potter!"

"Will you come and talk at my school, Mama?" Juanita pleaded. "Artie Torres's daddy came and talked, and all he did was skydive."

"We'll see," Mom said. "Let's all take it one step at a time."

"And in the meantime, we shall have a feast," *Abuela* announced. "I made *quesadillas*, with everything on them."

At school on Monday, Ernesto wondered whether Naomi and Clay would arrive together as usual. Their argument had been pretty bitter. He wondered whether they'd made up. Each time a student came into Ms. Hunt's class, he turned to see if they were there. Clay missed classes occasionally, but Naomi never did. So when Ms. Hunt started class and neither Naomi or Clay were in their seats, Ernesto started to worry. He feared that their argument outside the

Zamora house on Friday had grown worse. Maybe something awful had happened.

"Today, my dears," Ms. Hunt began, "we have the test you've all been looking forward to. So sharpen your wits. I am going to find out, when I see your tests, how much attention you have been paying to the adventures of Macbeth and his lady."

If Clay missed this test, he could lose his academic eligibility to play football. Ernesto thought for sure that the test would force him to attend class, no matter what had gone wrong.

As Ms. Hunt passed out the tests, she warned, "Remember, no cheating. Any cheating will result in an automatic F. No argument will do you a bit of good."

Ernesto had studied hard for the test, and he felt he had a good grasp on *Macbeth*. But Naomi's not being present was distracting him. His mind went down numerous dark alleys, all fearful possibilities. Ernesto forced himself to focus on the test on the desk before him.

The first question: "Why is Macbeth described as a tragic figure? Cite examples. Explain why he was called someone with moral inconsistency." Ernesto began writing. He described the agony of soul that Macbeth suffered as he slipped into mental darkness. Macbeth knew right from wrong. When he chose evil over good, his choice destroyed him. The second question dealt with Lady Macbeth. Ernesto found it easy to answer. He felt he'd grasped the personality of this troubled woman.

Ernesto was happy with his responses to the questions. He thought he'd make a good grade. He had As in science and history. With an A in English, he'd nail a good junior year. Ernesto had earned good marks in the school in Los Angeles, and he was doing the same here at Cesar Chavez High.

But . . . where was Naomi?

When the bell rang ending class, Ms. Hunt picked up the tests. "I will work diligently to have these back to you by Wednesday," she promised. "I hope you all

139

did well. We certainly spent a lot of time on *Macbeth*."

Abel Ruiz walked out with Ernesto. Abel was not as good a student as Ernesto, but he had a solid B minus. "I think I did okay," he assured himself, "but it was hard."

"Yeah, it was a tough test," Ernesto agreed. He didn't want to make Abel feel badly by telling the truth—that he thought the test was pretty easy if you'd studied.

"Abel," he continued, "I'm worried about Naomi. She never misses class, especially when there's an important test."

"I noticed old Clay was missing in action too," Abel noted. "I hope they didn't do something stupid like run off together. They're pretty hot and heavy."

Ernesto felt ill for a moment. Maybe Naomi and Clay had a big reconciliation and they *did* go off together somewhere. Naomi told Ernesto that she loved Clay. Would she do something as stupid, though, as eloping?

"Friday night at Tessie Zamora's homecoming party Naomi and Clay had a big argument," Ernesto told him.

"Maybe Clay arranged a big weekend to make up for it," Abel suggested. "I overheard them planning to go into the mountains and snowboard the minute there's enough of the white stuff. Listen, Ernie, you gotta stop obsessing about the chick. She's crazy for Clay Aguirre. She's as hooked on him as dopeheads are hooked on crack and meth. He makes her stupid. The chick is a lost cause, I'm tellin' you."

They walked off to their next classes.

At lunchtime, Ernesto called Naomi on her cell phone. He was transferred to voice mail. Either she wasn't there, or she wasn't taking calls. Ernesto then called the land-line phone at the Martinez house. He hoped he wouldn't get Felix Martinez. Fortunately, Naomi's mom answered.

"Hi, this is Ernie Sandoval, Mrs. Martinez," Ernesto introduced himself. "I'm kinda worried about Naomi. She wasn't in

141

class today, and she missed a big test. That's uh . . . not like her."

"Yes," Mrs. Martinez replied, "she's home sick."

"Nothing serious, I hope?" Ernesto asked.

"No, she'll be okay," Mrs. Martinez told him. "She just didn't feel like going to school. Maybe the teacher will give her a makeup test." There was something strange about her voice. Ernesto had a sneaking suspicion that she was lying.

"Ms. Hunt, our English teacher, she's really tough," Ernesto advised. "When students miss a test, she wants a doctor's report or something to prove they were really too sick to come in."

"Okay, we'll try to get the doctor to . . . you know . . ." Mrs. Martinez responded, "write something . . ." Her voice trailed off.

When he closed his cell phone, Ernesto wasn't reassured. Naomi was a strong girl. She wouldn't let a headache or a little stomach ache keep her from class. In the month that Ernesto had been attending Chavez, he couldn't remember when Naomi missed school.

More dark worries swarmed in Ernesto's mind. What happened after Clay's Mustang pulled away from the Zamora house on Friday night? Clay seemed on the verge of slapping Naomi before Ernesto intervened. The confrontation didn't come to violence, Ernesto firmly believed, only because he yelled and then Fernando and Rosalie came out. They defused the situation. But what about afterward? Did the arguing continue? When Naomi was alone in the car with Clay, did he do what he'd intended to do outside the Zamora house? Was she hurt?

Ernesto thought about Naomi the rest of the day. He couldn't get her off his mind. He was starting to care a lot for her. If she actually loved Clay and he was decent to her, then Ernesto knew he could move on. He would be sad, but he could handle his disappointment. But what tore him apart was that Naomi was in a bad relationship. And, as Abel Ruiz said, she was as helpless as a drug addict.

Right after classes ended, Ernesto got into his Volvo and headed for Naomi's house.

CHAPTER EIGHT

Ernesto the Martinez driveway. Zack's Honda was gone. Apparently he had gotten it working again. Ernesto considered the possibility that Naomi wasn't home, that she was gone somewhere with Clay. Naomi probably would resent Ernesto's coming here and checking up on her. She might even get mad. Ernesto didn't care. He knew he had no right to be checking up on the girl, but he had to. He wasn't her boyfriend. He wasn't anything to her, but still he was so worried that he had to make sure she was okay.

When Ernesto reached the screen door, Brutus started barking ferociously. "It's okay," Ernesto spoke to him through the closed door. "It's only me."

"Brutus, stop it!" Naomi's voice came from the back of the house. Ernesto was a little relieved. She was home, and she sounded all right. That eased his main worries, but he needed to talk to her. "Stop barking, Brutus! Who's there?" Naomi called out.

"It's me, Ernie Sandoval, Naomi," Ernesto called back.

"Oh. Hi Ernie!" she waved as she came from the back of the house and opened the screen door. "I missed the test, huh? I guess I'll have to throw myself on the mercy of Ms. Hunt when I get back to school. I think she'll let me make up the test." Naomi sounded fine. She didn't sound sick at all.

"Naomi, can I come in for a minute?" Ernesto asked.

"Uh, Brutus is running loose," she advised.

"Naomi," Ernesto pleaded, "I'm worried about you, okay? Just put the dog in the den, and let me come in for a minute. Okay?"

146

"Ernie," Naomi protested, "I have this nasty bug. I don't want you to get near me and catch it. You better just go home."

"Okay," Ernesto acceded. Turning away, he yelled, "See you in school."

He pretended to be walking away from the door. After several seconds, Naomi peered out, to make sure he was gone. When she saw Ernie, her right hand flew to her face to cover her ugly black eye.

Naomi Martinez tried to cover her injury, but she was too late.

"That piece of trash hit you, didn't he?" Ernesto swung around to face her and insisted bitterly.

"Take it easy, Ernie," Naomi said in a cool, soft voice.

"You gonna lie to me, Naomi? You gonna say you ran into a door or something?" Ernesto demanded. "Don't bother, 'cause I'm not buying that."

"No, I'm not going to tell you I ran into a door, Ernie," Naomi assured him. "Clay punched me in the face. We're finished,

147

Ernie. We broke up. It's over. He begged me to forgive him. He's devastated, but I won't forgive him. I told him that. He can't deal with it. He said he felt so terrible he was quitting the football team and maybe dropping out of Chavez too. I told him I didn't care. I just don't want anything to do with him anymore." Naomi's voice quivered a little, but she had a determined look in her eyes.

"He should be arrested for doing that," Ernesto told her.

"No, I don't want anything like that, Ernie," Naomi objected. "Don't even go there. If you call the cops, I'd just deny it ever happened. I'd say I ran into a door. I don't want to hurt Clay. I don't want to ruin his life. It's just over for us. I'm going to put it behind me. I'm going to school tomorrow, and I'm telling Ms. Hunt I had this accident. I got hurt, and I was dizzy and stuff so I couldn't come to school. I think I can take the makeup test."

Naomi walked into the house, and Ernesto followed her. She poured two cups of coffee, which was brewed in a pot on the stove, and they sat at the kitchen table. Naomi took big, nervous gulps of coffee. She looked as though she was on the verge of crying.

"Is there anything I can do, Naomi?" Ernesto asked.

"Yeah, just be my friend like you've been, Ernie," she responded. "You know, I've seen my mom put up with a lot of garbage over the years, but Dad never hit her. He yelled and stomped around, and a couple times he threatened her. But he never hit her. I know it's been hard for her, especially when he's been drinking. But, you know, there've been good times too, really good times."

She took another big gulp of coffee and continued talking. "We go camping in the summer, sometimes even to Big Bear in the winter. Dad is nicer then. He's sorta like a kid again. I mean, I guess I thought guys are nasty sometimes and say ugly things. But if deep down they love you, then they

won't actually *hit* you. I never saw it coming, Ernie. I thought Clay was like Dad,
kind of a boor . . . kind of mean sometimes.
But I never thought he'd punch me in the
face. I just never believed it could happen."

Naomi finished her coffee and took a
deep, shuddering breath. She closed her
eyes, then opened them again.

"Ernie, thanks for being worried about
me. Thanks for stopping by and caring
enough to check up on me. But I'm okay. I
really am okay. They say what doesn't kill
you makes you stronger, right? Well, I hope
I'm stronger now." She tried to smile, but
she didn't quite pull it off. Ernesto could
tell she wanted him to leave. He nodded
to her, went out to his Volvo, and drove to
work.

On the way to the pizzeria, Ernesto
couldn't get Naomi off his mind. He could
tell she was hurting, and not just from the
black eye. *Mostly* not from the black eye.
She and Clay had been together since middle school. She told Ernesto that she loved

him, and she probably still did. But she was being smart in seeing the handwriting on the wall. If she stayed with Clay Aguirre, she would be starting a long, bad trip. Guys like him could apologize and swear to do better, but, when their rage kicked in again, all bets were off.

As he was working the counter that night, he heard loud giggling. Soon several girls appeared. One of them, Rosalie Rivas, was pushing Tessie in her wheelchair. Fernando Sanchez was right behind her. Several other cheerleaders were in the group.

"Wow, you guys!" Tessie was saying. "You don't know how much I missed pizza! That hospital food is for the birds. I mean, I guess it's nutritious and stuff, but ewww! I want pepperoni pizza and lots of cheese, the works." Then Tessie spotted Ernesto. "Oh wow, do you work here, Ernie?" she cried.

"Yeah," Ernesto replied, smiling at the girl.

"You look so cute in your striped shirt, Ernie," Tessie giggled.

"Thanks," Ernesto said. "I'm glad you're getting out with your friends."

The group gathered at a large table with wheelchair access in the corner. Ernesto overheard Tessie say, "I called Naomi and asked her to come. I thought she and Clay would be here for sure. Naomi's been so great. She visited me tons of times in the hospital."

"I guess she's sick," another girl suggested. "I didn't see her in school today."

Ernesto thought that, tomorrow at school, everybody would know Naomi's dark little secret.

Rosalie was helping Tessie cut her pizza when Tessie laughed and protested. "Rosie, you've done enough for me! I got a busted leg, but my hands work fine!" Then Tessie looked at the others, "Rosie has been my angel through all this."

Ernesto glanced at Rosalie Rivas. Her blonde hair kept falling over her face, and she kept pushing it back. She was a very pretty girl, but Carmen had been right about her. She looked so sad. Even her smile seemed fake.

The girls sat for while. Then Fernando showed up to see Rosalie. When they took a table by themselves, the girls left.

After work that night, Ernesto was walking to his Volvo. He saw Fernando's red Honda parked in the far corner of the lot, not too far away. It was dark, but he saw two figures in the front seat, with the windows open—probably Fernando and Rosalie. Ernesto shrugged and figured they were getting some hugs and kisses in.

Then he heard Rosalie sobbing loudly. Fernando had his arm around the girl, and he seemed to be consoling her. Something was wrong all right, something big. Maybe one of Rosalie's parents was seriously sick or something. Some people didn't want to share stuff like that, even with their friends. Ernesto figured that, if anybody could help Rosalie, Fernando could. She was closer to him than she was to anyone else. So Ernesto got in his Volvo and drove home.

When Ernesto came through the door at home, Mom was working hard on her book revisions. *Abuela* was reading to the girls in their room. Dad was reading in the living room. He asked Ernesto whether he knew where Naomi Martinez was. "She missed my history class," Dad told him, "and all her other classes too. The school office couldn't get her parents."

"Yeah," Ernesto replied. "I went to her house to check on her. She's okay. She'll be in school tomorrow. Dad . . . she doesn't want everybody to know how it happened, but she's got a black eye. I guess a lot of kids will guess, but . . ."

"Clay Aguirre hit her?" Dad stormed, an angry look in his eyes.

"Yeah," Ernesto answered.

"Did Naomi call the police?" Luis Sandoval asked, his angry look hardening. "I hope she did."

"No, Dad," Ernesto responded, "she doesn't want to do that. She said if anybody called the police, she'd just deny everything. She doesn't want to make trouble for Aguirre. But she said she's through with him. She told me they broke up for good."

"That's a good thing," Dad declared. "I hope she sticks to her word. Clay Aguirre needs to get help with anger management, though. He's just a boy. If he keeps blowing up like that without getting a handle on his emotions, he'll turn into a violent adult. He could even turn into a criminal."

"He told Naomi he's quitting the football team," Ernesto reported, "and maybe dropping out of school too. He says he feels really bad about what happened"

"I hope he doesn't drop out of school," Dad said, sincerely concerned. "That would be just compounding the tragedy."

At school the next day, Ernesto lingered near the front mural of Cesar Chavez. Naomi usually came by this way on her way to English. He hoped she'd keep her promise and return to school. It would be awful if her embarrassment over the black eye ruined her excellent grade point average.

Fernando Sanchez came along by himself. On the spur of the moment, Ernesto approached him. "Is Rosalie okay?" he inquired. "She's looking so sad these days. Her friends are worried about her."

Fernando got a strange look on his face. It wasn't anger, but an uncomfortable look, like he was not about to talk about Rosalie's problems. "We all got problems, man. She's okay," he responded.

"I was just wondering if there was anything we could do," Ernesto persisted. "Rosie has been so good about helping Tessie. I mean, if she needs any help, we'd all be glad to—"

"She's fine," Fernando asserted. "Tessie's accident got her down a lot. But now that Tessie's doing better, Rosie's gonna be okay too. Gotta go man." He turned and walked off.

Then Naomi Martinez came riding up on her bicycle. Her black eye was not nearly as noticeable as it had been. It had faded, and she'd put on a lot of makeup. Naomi was wearing one of her beautiful red pullover sweaters, and she looked great. Even with a shiner, she was still the most beautiful girl at Cesar Chavez High School.

Ernesto stared at Naomi with his usual admiration, but he knew better than to move in on her. He had to let a decent interval go by before told her how he felt about her.

Ms. Hunt permitted Naomi Martinez to take a makeup test after school. Ms. Hunt knew her students well, and she knew Naomi would never skip a test day because she was not prepared to take the exam. In class that day, Ms. Hunt started work on the Greek play *Oedipus Rex*. "We will be studying the riddle of human suffering in this play," Ms. Hunt announced.

Ernesto kept glancing around to see whether Clay Aguirre would show up, but he never did. Maybe he was serious about dropping out of school. Ernesto knew Naomi well enough to know that his dropping out would make her feel sad and guilty. But he hoped it wouldn't change her resolve to stay away from him.

After school, Ernesto did some trial runs for Coach Muñoz. Even the coach noticed that Ernesto was distracted.

"Your time is off, Sandoval," Coach Muñoz noted. "What's with you? You look good, but you're not sharp. What's the problem?" Muñoz was pinning his hopes for raising the pathetic Chavez track team from the doldrums with Ernesto Sandoval and Julio Avila. This afternoon, Julio made Ernesto look awful. And Ernesto was so worried about Naomi that he didn't even care.

After practice, Ernesto plunked down in his Volvo but didn't go home, even though he had a lot do. He felt too unsettled to go home. Just then, Carmen Ibarra walked by.

"Hi, Ernie," she hailed. "I'm gonna get a taco. Wanna come along?"

Now *that* sounded like a good idea. Ernesto was out of the car again, and they started over to Hortencia's.

"What are you doing hanging around the school so late," he asked Carmen.

"Your dad's helping me with some stuff in his class," she responded. "He's such a nice man, Ernie."

"I agree," Ernesto beamed.

As they were munching their tacos, Rosalie Rivas came into the shop alone.

"Hey Rosie," Carmen yelled, "come sit with us."

Rosalie brought her iced coffee over and sat down. "Hi," she said glumly. Her eyes seemed shadowed.

"Rosie, we're worried about you," Carmen told her. "Is everything okay at home? Your mom or dad aren't sick, are they? We're all friends, Rosie. You need to share if something's bothering you."

"I'm okay," Rosalie said. "My parents both work, and they're gone all the time. But I'm used to that."

"You sure we can't help you with something?" Carmen persisted. "I mean, you used to laugh more than anybody, and now I never see you laughing. Rosie, we been friends since we were babies. You can tell me anything. You can tell Ernie too. We care about you, girl."

Rosalie started to cry. "I just got the blues. I mean, I feel sad and stuff, but it'll be okay." She gulped down her iced coffee and got up. She didn't seem to want to talk anymore. She hurried from the restaurant and vanished down the street.

"That girl is going down for the count, Ernie," Carmen commented in a deeply worried voice. "Something is tearing her apart." Carmen and Ernie got up. "Let's follow her," Carmen suggested, "I got a terrible feeling she's not going home."

CHAPTER NINE

As Ernesto and Carmen walked, Ernesto remarked, "You're right, Carmen. She's not headed for her house. She seems to be going toward the park."

"A lot of weirdoes hang out there," Ernesto noted. "You don't think she's doing drugs or something."

"I don't know, Ernie, but there's something going on," Carmen said. "Something she can't talk about."

Rosalie kept on walking until she reached the park that included a ravine and a lake. A lot of eucalyptus trees stood around the lake, and it was home to ducks, Canada geese in the winter, and even a few pelicans who strayed from the bay.

Carmen and Ernesto followed at a distance. Rosalie never once looked back and saw them.

"She's like a zombie," Carmen commented worriedly.

Rosalie walked to the water's edge and stood there. Ernesto thought she might feed the ducks, but she made no move to do so. She just stood there, looking into the water. She hung her head, and her shoulders heaved, as if she were crying.

"We gotta do something," Ernesto urged. "We gotta tell her parents to get help for her."

"Yeah," Carmen agreed.

"She's going in the water!" Ernesto yelled.

Ernesto and Carmen rushed to where Rosalie was wading into the shallow part of the lake where there were reeds.

"Rosie!" Carmen shouted. "What are you doing!?"

Rosalie turned, shocked, as if she'd been caught doing something bad. "I was just . . . " she stammered.

162

Carmen and Ernesto waded toward Rosalie, took hold of her, and led her toward the shore. "Come on, girl," Carmen commanded. "Let's sit on the grass under the eucalyptus trees and talk."

The three of them sat down. Rosalie stared straight ahead, and she spoke in a dull monotone. "I did something terrible. Nobody knows what I did except for Fernando. I'm so ashamed. If you guys knew what I did, you would hate me forever."

Carmen put her arm around Rosalie's shoulders and consoled her. "I would never *ever* hate you, Rosalie. There's nothing you could have done that would make me stop being your friend. We're *hermanas*, girl. Ernie is your friend too. We just want to help you."

Rosalie was quiet for a while, as if taking in what Carmen had to say. Then she started speaking.

"Fernando drank too much that night," Rosalie began. "He drinks too much a lot, and then he drives. But he's my boyfriend, and I love him. And he loves me too. Sometimes he yells at the kids in the street, but he's not mean. He's just a little *loco* sometimes. We went to a party. One of the guys boosted a lot of booze from the supermarket. Everybody was drinking a lot, but I wasn't 'cause liquor makes me sick."

Rosalie went on. "So everybody was getting really buzzed. It was like dusk when we left the party. Fernando was so drunk that he had to lean on me when we walked, or he woulda fallen down. I had to go home, and Fernando said he'd drive me. But he was so drunk he almost fell down getting in the car. I'd never seen him so drunk. So I told him to sit in the back of the Honda and I'd drive."

Ernesto and Carmen looked at each other, fearing what was coming but not saying anything. Rosalie had to get it out. She had to share what happened because keeping it locked inside was eating her alive.

"Fernando," she continued, "he got in back, and he like passed out. I turned the key and started the car. I had no driver's license. I didn't hardly know how to drive a car. But a couple times my father let me go down the street when nobody was on the road. I thought I could do it." Tears began running down Rosalie's face.

Carmen tightened her arm round Rosalie's shoulder.

"The car, it kinda stalled at first. I wish it never had started, but it did. I got it moving. I thought I could get us home. It was kinda foggy and getting dark. I drove down Caldwell. I don't know how fast I was going, but I heard a thud. I thought I'd hit a bump in the road or something."

Rosalie started to cry convulsively. She sobbed as she went on. "I didn't . . . know . . . what I hit. I was so scared. I looked back and people . . . people were running into the street . . . a lotta people and screaming . . . I didn't know why they were screaming. I was . . . so . . . scared. I just kept going. I wanted to get home. I thought it'd be okay . . . if I just got home."

Rosalie started to collect herself. She was no longer sobbing. "I got Fernando home. He lives one block from me. I left the car there and I ran to my house. I ran so fast. I stumbled and I fell. I was crying because I didn't know what I hit. I thought maybe it was a dog."

Rosalie buried her face in her hands, sucked in a deep breath, and began sobbing all over again. "It was the news . . . I hit . . . I hit . . . Tessie . . . and I wanted to die!"

"Ohhh," Carmen moaned, holding the girl in her arms.

"Fernando knew what happened," Rosalie cried. "I told him. He said it wasn't my fault . . . he said he'd take care of it. He brought the Honda to out of town to get it fixed and painted and stuff. Fernando has a cousin in the next town. He took care of everything. Fernando's parents, they never knew. They thought we'd hit a tree or something. Nobody knew. Just me and Fernando. He kept telling me it wasn't my fault. I didn't want for it to happen."

Rosalie rocked back and forth for a while. "I didn't even know I'd hit Tessie, or I woulda stopped. I swear it. Fernando said we had to keep it a secret. We'd be in terrible trouble, and confessing wouldn't help Tessie. Oh, you guys, I love Tessie! I love her like a sister. I wish I'd been the one hit instead of her. I'd do anything to make it all go away." Rosalie moaned.

"Have you said anything to your parents?" Carmen asked.

"No. Not a word," Rosalie sobbed. "I was too afraid."

"Rosie, you gotta tell your parents," Carmen commanded. "You can't keep this to yourself."

"I'm so thankful that Tessie is getting better, but it haunts me,' Rosalie cried. "In the middle of the night, I'll have a nightmare and I'll feel the . . . the thud. And I'll start crying,."

"Rosie, I know your parents," Carmen assured her. "They're good people. They'll help you through this."

"But I'll be in terrible trouble. I'll go to prison and stuff," Rosalie objected.

"No!" Ernesto said decisively. "You're only sixteen years old, Rosie. You didn't know you had hit someone until later. You didn't deliberately leave someone injured in the street. You didn't even know what happened until later. You weren't even driving drunk. It was just a horrible mistake. They take care of stuff like this in juvenile court. They don't even give out the names of the kid. You'll probably be on probation, and you won't get a driver's license anytime soon. But you'll get through this."

"If you don't tell the truth, Rosie," Carmen told her, "this will *always* torture you. You'll always be worrying that the dark secret will come out."

Rosalie looked up at Carmen and Ernesto. She blinked through her tears. "Will you guys come with me when I tell my parents?"

"You bet I will," Carmen said.

"Me too," Ernesto added. "I'll tell them how you've been helping Tessie so much. You've been an angel to her."

The three teenagers rode to Rosalie's house in Ernesto's Volvo. They told Rosalie's parents the whole story, filling in when Rosalie was crying too much to be understood. Rosalie's mother cried, and her father looked shocked and angry. Then he cried too. By the time Carmen and Ernesto left, the parents were embracing their daughter.

One of Luis Sandoval's brothers, Arturo Sandoval, was a lawyer in the *barrio*. He was well respected as a compassionate *abogado*. Rosalie's father called him immediately—that afternoon—and the whole family was going to his office the following afternoon. They called Fernando Sanchez and his parents, and they agreed to go as well.

When Ernie got home after school the next day, he got a call from Naomi. "Ernie, could you give me a ride over to Tessie's house?"

"Sure," Ernesto replied eagerly. Any chance to help Naomi Martinez delighted him. He was slowly, very slowly building up the courage to ask her out.

When Naomi was in the car, she explained, "Rosalie called me and told me everything, Ernie. Isn't that just the saddest thing in the world? She was just trying to keep Fernando from driving drunk, and look what happened."

"Yeah," Ernesto agreed. "Rosalie is a good person. She would have stopped if she'd known she hit somebody. I think she'll be okay. She was released to the custody of her parents when the police learned what happened. My *Tío* Arturo, he's a good lawyer. He'll help things come out right. There's plenty of blame to go around in what happened. Fernando shouldn't have gotten drunk when he knew Rosie wasn't even a driver. And Rosalie, well, she shouldn't have gotten behind the wheel.

And Tessie never should have run out into the street in the middle of the block, especially in the dusk and fog."

When they pulled into the Zamora driveway, several cars were already there. The Rivas family had brought Rosalie, and Fernando's parents had come too.

As the walked up the driveway, Naomi said, half to herself, "I'm so glad Rosalie called me. She said she just needed someone to be there with her."

Ernest nodded that he understood and agreed. He was glad too.

When Ernesto and Naomi walked in, Tessie and Rosalie were holding hands. "She forgave me," Rosalie cried. The tears started again, but this time she looked like her old self. The darkness had lifted. There were no more dark secrets.

"It wasn't your fault, Rosie," Tessie consoled her. "We all messed up that night, and it was just a horrible accident. Even if you had realized you hit somebody and stopped, it wouldn't have made any difference in my injuries. But I'm doing good now. I'm gonna be okay, Rosie, and so are you."

Mr. and Mrs. Rivas were talking quietly with Tessie's and Fernando's parents. The conversation was cordial. They were all good and decent people, caught up in a tragedy involving their children. Nobody wanted to cast stones.

Naomi hugged Tessie and Rosalie. Naomi's black eye was even less noticeable than the day before.

When Ernesto and Naomi were back in the Volvo, Naomi took a deep breath. "Just goes to show what can happen when you're driving or even walking if you're not careful. It could have been so much worse. What if Tessie had died?" Naomi shuddered.

Ernesto did not mention Clay Aguirre or that he was missing from school. But Naomi brought it up, as they pulled away from the Zamoras' house. "Clay lost his eligibility to play sports, at least for a while.

His grades were sinking even before he missed the test in Ms. Hunt's room. I ran into Clay's cousin, and she told me."

"You okay with what's going on, Naomi?" Ernesto asked. He was being cautious. He wanted to know whether she was handling her ending of the relationship with Clay well or was hurting a lot. But he didn't know how to phrase the question.

"Not really," Naomi replied evasively. "But it is what it is. I guess I still love him. You can't turn something like that off like you shut off a faucet. I remember so many good times we had. He's fun, he really is. He can be awful, but he can be nice and sweet too. We've been friends since fourth grade and sorta a couple since middle school. That's like eight years. That's half my life. You can't just wipe all that away, Ernie."

"I understand," Ernesto said, though he really didn't. He never loved a girl so deeply that losing her would have given him such pain as Naomi was going through. He liked Gabriella up in Los Angeles, but their relationship was nothing profound for either of them. Ernesto thought he might be able to fall in love with Naomi. He felt that strongly about her. He thought about her a lot. But he didn't think he was in love with her yet . . . not yet. He was getting close, though. He wasn't sure how things would go, and he was afraid of getting as close as he wanted to be.

"Ernie," Naomi blurted, "did you ever love a girl?"

"Uh . . . I've had feelings," Ernesto admitted. "I'm not sure what to call them."

"Be careful, Ernie," Naomi advised. "Love hurts. It can hurt like anything. It's bad when you love somebody and then it's over." She closed her eyes as if she might cry, but she didn't.

"Life has a way of mocking you," she mused ruefully. "You want to remember all the good reasons you have for breaking up with somebody you love. You want to keep on feeling angry. Then all you can think of is that night at Big Bear just before Christmas, when you and him snuggled together around the campfire and the snowflakes were coming down, big and soft, not enough to douse the fire, but just magical. And he leaned over and kissed you, and you thought you'd died and gone to Heaven. And you could never be quite that happy again in a million years."

"Don't weaken," Ernesto murmured under his breath. He did not dare say it out loud to Naomi. She seemed right on the edge, torn by the happy memories, less and less willing to give up something that had meant so much to her. "Don't weaken, girl," he said again without her hearing. "If you do, it will all happen again, and again. You know that's true. And all the nice memories can't change that."

They were near Naomi's house. Naomi sighed and admitted, "I guess it would never work, huh? I can't live my life like that, always being afraid I'd said the wrong thing. Looking at him and wondering if he was mad—if he was *really* mad. I want to feel safe with somebody, no matter what I say, no matter even if we're arguing and stuff. I want to feel safe."

Ernesto said nothing as he pulled into her driveway, but he was relieved. Her common sense was prevailing, at least for now. Maybe at other times of crisis she'd doubt herself again, but she was a strong girl, a smart girl. Ernesto relied on her smarts to get her through.

Naomi's father, Felix Martinez, was in the driveway. He moved over as Ernesto pulled in. His son Zack and the pit bull were running around. Zack was throwing a ball, and Brutus was leaping into the air, catching it. They all seemed to be having a good time. Naomi laughed a little. "Look at Dad. He's like a teenager when he's with Brutus. He had a dog like that when he was a kid. He's had a lot of dogs since, but he said Brutus is most like the dog he had when he was a kid."

The front door opened, and Linda Martinez was standing there, framed in the doorway. "It's getting dark, you guys," she called out. "Dinner is on the table. I don't want it to get cold. Come on in." She spotted Ernesto. "You're welcome to join us, Ernie. I made *arroz con pollo*, and there's enough for an army."

"No thanks," Ernesto declined. "But it sure smells good!"

Felix Martinez, Zack, and Naomi headed for the door, but Brutus led the way, bounding ahead of everybody else. Maybe he smelled the chicken too. Ernesto watched nervously as the dog approached Mrs. Martinez. Ernesto expected her to get out of his way quickly, but she didn't move. Brutus shoved past her, bumping into her legs. The woman didn't flinch.

Ernesto was astonished.

Naomi had not yet gone into the house. Ernesto said to her, "Did you see that? Your mom just let Brutus bump against her."

Naomi smiled. "Mom isn't afraid of him anymore. He really is a good dog. He's a big, lovable white dog. It's so weird how scared she was in the beginning. But, it's true, Ernie. It's not the breed that defines a dog. It's the breeder. Brutus was never beaten up or abused. So he's nice. All he's ever known is love."

"Yeah," Ernesto agreed. "That's what Mom is trying to say in that book she's writing. You can't put dogs or people in a box because of how they look. But you gotta take time to know their hearts."

Naomi paused before going in the front door. "Brutus is nice. You're nice too, Ernie. I haven't known you long, just a little over a month. But I trust you so much. I don't know anybody I trust more. I wouldn't think twice about asking you for a favor. That says a lot about your heart, Ernesto Sandoval."

Naomi smiled at Ernesto and finally went in the house to get some of that fragrant *arroz con pollo*. Ernie stood there a few seconds before he got back into his Volvo. He let her compliment resonate in his mind and heart. It made him feel good. It made him feel on top of the world. The compliment didn't mean Naomi Martinez was falling in love with Ernesto. It didn't mean that at all. It didn't even mean she might eventually fall in love with him.

All it meant was that she liked him and that she trusted him. But that wasn't half bad as a beginning. Once Mom told Ernesto that the most endearing quality Luis Sandoval had had when they first met was that she trusted him. "I never could have given my heart to a boy I didn't trust," Mom said.

Ernesto was still smiling when he got into the Volvo and headed for home. He turned on the radio and put on some hot salsa music. He was tapping his fingers on the steering wheel. He turned up the volume. Ernesto wondered whether he *was* falling in love with Naomi Martinez. He was excited and frightened. He thought, "Is this what love feels like? Being on a roller coaster and you're going higher and higher. The sky is so close you swear, if you reached out, you could touch it?"

On Thursday morning, Ms. Hunt returned the corrected tests as she'd promised. Ernesto knew he had done well, but he wasn't sure how well. Naomi's absence on the day of the test had distracted him. That might have dropped him down a notch.

When Ms. Hunt placed the test, face down, on Ernesto's desk, she smiled at him. He turned the paper over quickly and saw a big A. It also had a written comment: "You turned in the best essays of anybody in this class. Way to go, Ernesto!"

Ernesto had decided not to drive to school that morning. So when classes were over and it was time to go home, the Volvo wasn't waiting for him in the parking lot. He planned to jog home. He needed to get in all the running he could to help Coach Muñoz finally win a meet for his team.

As Ernesto was leaving the campus, he saw Fernando Sanchez standing alone under a eucalyptus tree. Ernesto stopped and greeted him. "How's it going, man?"

"We're hangin' in there," Fernando replied. "Rosalie has a court appearance. We think she'll get probation. I've got some legal stuff to deal with for getting the car fixed up to cover up, you know. But we'll get through it. You probably saw the story in the news. At least we weren't mentioned by name."

Fernando reflected for a few seconds, then spoke. "It's a bad patch, but it'll be okay. I'm off the booze, man. *He terminado*. Done. Finished. I'm seventeen man, and I'm an *alcohólico*. But no more . . . never. *He terminado!*"

CHAPTER TEN

On Saturday morning, Ernesto checked himself out in the mirror after doing his weightlifting. He could see the difference in himself when he looked at his upper body. He was definitely more muscular, more ripped. He thought he looked better than ever. He was still a slender guy. He wouldn't be offering Fernando Sanchez or Clay Aguirre any competition on the football field. But he still felt great about himself. He thought, "If I visited my old school in Los Angeles, my friends would say, 'Hey man, what happened to you?'" Ernesto felt stronger too. His running was improved. He knew he was going to give his rival, Julio Avila, a run for his money.

Later at the breakfast table, Mom said, "Janet is shopping my manuscript around. We ought to know in a few weeks if a publisher likes it enough to take it on. I'm not getting my hopes up too high, but Janet said everybody in the office loves it." Mom grinned and poured more syrup on her pancakes. Mom ate more than anybody else in the Sandoval household. But she had a lot of nervous energy that burned up the calories. She was always running around doing something. Ernesto rarely saw her just sitting.

Luis Sandoval talked about his special project at Cesar Chavez High School. He was luring the *barrio* dropouts and wannabe gang members back to school. He was trying to keep the kids in school until they graduated. And he also wanted to get the dropouts back. So he donned a baseball cap and put on a T-shirt and jeans. Then he strolled around the neighborhood starting up conversations with kids who seemed aimless. Wearing a dress shirt and tie in the

183

classroom, Ernesto's father looked mature. But he looked young enough in informal clothes to pass for a twenty-something. That gave him some clout with kids. Dad knew their music and their language, and the kids identified with him. They listened when he told them about kids who came to tragic ends when he was in high school.

"There's a new student coming to my American history class next week," Dad announced at the breakfast table. "She was a gang girl for a while, but she's got a lot of potential. I went over to her parents' house and talked to her. Her mother speaks only Spanish. The girl doesn't write well in English, but she's working on her skills. She's an intelligent girl. I explained to her mother that she could have a bright future if she returned to school. The mother is a fine person. She wants the best for her child. She understands that dropping out of school is like slamming the door on a good life. So Yvette will be coming to Cesar Chavez High."

Ernesto looked up. "Not Yvette Ozono," he remarked. Ernesto and her father had met the girl under tragic circumstances. Her new boyfriend was a good kid named Tommy Alvarado, who was in one of Dad's history classes. Tommy was gunned down by Yvette's gang boyfriend, Coyote. Coyote wasn't willing to give up his girlfriend, and he killed Tommy at Yvette's birthday party. Yvette was so distraught about what happened that she told Ernesto and his father that she wanted to die. She wished she were in the coffin with Tommy.

"Yes, Yvette Ozono," Dad replied with a smile. Though Dad did not know Tommy Alvarado well, he delivered the boy's eulogy at Our Lady of Guadalupe Church. That act had touched Yvette's heart very much and had given Luis Sandoval an in with her.

"She's very nervous," Dad continued, "because she hasn't been in school for a long time. But I've lined up a senior girl to tutor her, and I'm available after school to help her

185

all I can. I've recruited my best and most friendly students to make Yvette feel like she's been at Chavez for a long time. Naomi Martinez and Carmen Ibarra are going to make sure to eat lunch with her and take her to the hangouts, like Hortencia's, after school. Tessie's family got her one of those self-propelled wheelchairs. So Tessie's going to be in school helping out too. The 'Welcome Back, Yvette' strategy is underway. All the girls know what a terrible tragedy Yvette suffered when she lost Tommy. They're all going to help." When Dad was finished speaking, he seemed very happy.

"Have I told you lately, *Señor* Sandoval, how very proud I am of you?" Mom told him with a big smile.

"*Señora* Sandoval," he responded, "I could not do so much without the support of the most wonderful wife in the world."

"I am so glad I picked you, Luis," Mom giggled.

"*Ay!*" Dad exclaimed, "I was under the impression that *I* picked *you*, Maria!"

"I was in love with you before you knew I existed, Luis," Mom admitted. She looked at Ernesto. "I saw him walking down the hall, and my heart started thumping. I was afraid he could hear it. Thumpa-da-thumpa-da. He never knew what hit him when Maria Vasquez went after him."

"Well, I am delighted that you decided to love me," Dad declared. "I couldn't believe it at first. How could this lovely girl love *me* when there were football heroes and boys who played the guitar all around."

The phone rang. When Mom answered it, her face showed pleasant surprise. "You guys coming down tomorrow? Oh that's great!" she cried. "You can have dinner with us."

Dad looked up, and Mom said, "My parents are coming down from LA. They'll be here three days. They're staying at a cousin's house, but they're coming here for dinner tomorrow."

"Wonderful!" Dad responded.

Maria Vasquez's parents never quite forgave Luis Sandoval for changing the course of their daughter's life. It was not so much Alfredo Vasquez, Maria's father, who was upset. Eva, her mother, had had grand dreams for her only child. The Vasquezes had no problem with Luis Sandoval, who was a fine, upstanding man from a good family with the highest of integrity. The problem was that their daughter had given up her plans to attend college and devoted herself to being a wife and mother. Maria Vasquez had been a straight-A honor student and the valedictorian of her class. She had been voted the student most likely to accomplish great things. Maria herself had planned to major in English in college. She had wanted to become a college professor and then a writer. Perhaps she would even enter politics and go to law school. But all that changed when she became Mrs. Luis Sandoval—mother and housewife.

Whenever Ernesto was with his grandmother, Eva Vasquez, he could see that she was still disappointed about her daughter's decision. She would say to Ernesto with a deep sigh, "Your mother was destined to be somebody."

Mom put down the phone and said, "We can have a nice leisurely dinner and catch up on everything."

Abuela Lena, who had been quietly eating her egg and cheese burrito loaded with salsa, offered to cook. "I will make my special chicken *enchiladas* for the occasion."

"No Mama," Ernesto's mother objected. "They don't eat Mexican food."

Abuela's eyebrows went up. "But they are Mexicans!" she cried.

"I know, Mama," Mrs. Sandoval explained, "but they've gotten away from the *tamales* and the *enchiladas*. Mom has always sort of fought a weight problem. So she's into salads and stuff. She worries about Dad too. He can't have his favorite— refried beans—anymore. I think I'll make a nice *ceviche*."

Abuela glanced at Ernesto and his two sisters. They all exchanged a look of disgust. *Abuela* recalled grimly, "I remember when they were at your wedding, Luis. They didn't like the Mexican music. They asked that nice mariachi trio to stop playing so they could put on canned music from some Broadway play."

"That was because one of the mariachi players was drunk, Mama," Ernesto's mother giggled. "He was Luis's friend from school, and he fell into the punch bowl."

"Poor Pedro," Dad recollected, shuddering and laughing at the same time.

Ernesto's grandfather was christened Alfredo Vasquez. But now everyone, other than his family of brothers and sisters, called him Al. Grandmother Vasquez was christened Evita, but now nobody could remember her ever being called that. She was Eva. To their many friends, most of them not Mexicans, they were Al and Eva.

The Vasquezes were lighter-skinned than the Sandovals. Though nobody came right out and said so, Ernesto always had the feeling that, in the minds of Eva and

Al, lighter was better than darker. Luis Sandoval had not only lured their gifted daughter from her shining career path. But he was also so dark that some impolite members of the Vasquez clan whispered, "*Indio*?"

Nevertheless, on Sunday when the Vasquezes arrived for dinner, they were warmly welcomed. Ernesto's mother hugged her parents. She loved them dearly, and they loved her.

The Vasquezes hugged their grandchildren, including Ernesto who was not crazy about being hugged by them. They shook hands with Luis Sandoval and warmly embraced his mother.

As the *ceviche* was being served, Ernesto's mother talked about Dad's plan to rescue neighborhood kids who had dropped out of school. "Sometimes Luis just walks around the street striking up conversations with kids," Mom said proudly. "He's convinced some of them to return to school."

Grandmother Eva frowned. "Isn't that dangerous, Luis?" she wondered. "I understand this *barrio* is now very crime ridden. You must be careful." Then, still looking at Dad, she went on. "Luis, don't you find your students here academically inferior to the ones you were teaching in Los Angeles?"

"Well," Dad responded, thoughtfully, "it's a poorer neighborhood, and the families are less proficient in English. So that does handicap the students. But we have a lot of great kids who are doing remarkably well too. It's really rewarding to see how they strive for excellence."

Grandma Eva looked wistful, almost angry, as she stabbed a shrimp with her fork. "You were such an achiever in school, Maria," she addressed her daughter. "Al and I were so proud of you. We imagined that one day you might teach English at Yale or Harvard, or perhaps be the CEO of a large company. Or go into politics. Remember how interested in world affairs you used to be?"

"I still am," Mom assured her. Then she decided to make her first announcement of the evening.

"Mama, Papa, I have good news," she declared breathlessly.

"You're going back to school?" *Abuela* beamed, holding her fork in front of her. She smiled broadly at her daughter.

"No, perhaps in time," Mom replied. "No, the news is that I am expecting a baby. I'm sure of it. And it will be a son. He will be called Alfredo. Not Al, but Alfredo."

Grandpa Alfredo was so delighted that tears ran down his face.

Abuela Eva's glowing smile flashed from her face. Her eyes darted briefly at Luis Sandoval and back to her daughter. Grandma was old herself again—sour.

"I'm very happy for you, of course," she said to her daughter. "I hope the added mouth does not put a strain on your budget. Your father and I cannot help much, but we will do what we can."

Perhaps, deep down, Mom had expected *Abuela's* reaction. She hid her disappointment as well as she could. But no one at the table missed it. Even though Katalina was only eight, she picked up on her mama's disappointment.

"Nana," she chirped, "Mama's written a book. And the agent is gonna sell it to some publisher. Then Mama will be famous like that Harry Potter lady."

Grandma Eva almost dropped a shrimp in her lap. She turned sharply and looked at her daughter. "You've written a book?" she asked.

In a few words, Katalina had changed the subject and the mood at the table.

Mom laughed self-consciously. "It's just a little children's book," she demurred. "Remember when I'd write those little pieces for magazines? Well, I wrote up this proposal for a book, and my agent is quite excited, but I don't know . . . "

"Mom writes really well," Ernesto chimed in.

"Well, I'm glad you've started writing again, darling," Grandma Eva said approvingly. "But don't hope for too much. Publishing is very competitive. It's hard to get a book published. I'm sure your book is a nice little thing, but . . . I mean, you have no background. If you were a college teacher . . . perhaps they would take you more seriously but . . . " She reached over and patted her daughter's hand. "If nothing comes of it, you can read your little story to the girls. I'm sure they'd enjoy it."

Eventually, the Vasquezes were putting on their coats and going toward the door. They promised to be back again soon, but now they were driving to the cousin's house in Julian.

When they left, Dad declared, "Well, that was nice."

"Yes, I'm always glad to see Mom and Dad," Mom said politely.

The next day, Monday, was a school holiday. Ernesto and his father were planning to begin sanding a bookcase when the phone rang.

Mom took the call and she began to gasp. "Really? Are you sure?" she cried. "Ohhh! Oh my goodness! Oh Janet, I love you, *love you*! Okay, I'll be waiting for it. Oh thank you, thank you!"

Mom put the phone down and screamed, "Janet found a publisher! The contracts are coming! They like my book. They're hiring an artist, and they really, *really* like it. And maybe I'll have to speak at bookstores and stuff."

Dad, Ernesto, *Abuela*, and the girls all hugged Mom. Mom and Dad danced around the living room like crazy teen-agers. Dad kept kissing Mom, and she kept screaming, "I'm so excited!"

Then, suddenly, Mom stopped in her tracks. She had a look of determination on her face. "My folks are still staying with my cousin," she said. "We have to go over there right now and deliver the news!"

"I'll warm up the minivan!" Dad announced, his finger pointed upward dramatically.

"Please let me drive," Ernesto volunteered. "I need the practice, and I'm a safe driver."

"Wonderful, *mi hijo*," Dad agreed. "Lead the way!"

They all piled into the minivan and headed for the house of Mama's cousin. They passed lush apple orchards before coming to the nice home where the Vasquez cousins lived.

"They'll be so surprised," Mom giggled as the van neared the house. "Mama said my book probably wouldn't be published. Ha! I could read it to you girls as a bedtime story!"

Katalina and Juanita laughed. "We still want you to read it to us, Mama!" Katalina cried.

They drove up and parked in the large circular driveway. Horses grazed in corrals in the back. The family was obviously well fixed.

Katalina insisted on running ahead and ringing the chiming doorbell. *Abuela* Eva came to the door, and she looked at the little girl in surprise. "Why, darling, what are you doing here?" she inquired.

Then Eva saw the others coming—Luis and his mother, followed by Juanita, Ernesto, and her daughter Maria.

"My goodness!" Eva Vasquez cried. "What is this all about?"

Maria Sandoval rushed to her mother and gave her a big hug. She hugged Grandpa Alfredo too, as he came up behind Eva. The Sandovals came into the house and gathered in the dining room for coffee. When everyone was seated, Mom leaned forward to speak. The Sandovals, knowing what she had to say, waited in silence. The others waited too, sensing an announcement.

"Last night," Mom addressed her cousins first, "I told my Mama and Papa the good news that we will be having a fourth child, a son."

Mom's cousins raised their hands and came over to kiss her. "*Muy bien*!" they told her several times.

"*Gracias*," she thanked them.

"But there is more," Mom continued. "My book will be published!" She paused to make sure of everyone's reaction. Mom's cousins didn't know she had written a book. They looked curious, wanting to know more. Mom's parents, especially *Abuela*, looked stunned.

"My agent just called me," Mom continued proudly. "She has found a publisher. They're getting the artist ready to make the illustrations, and I will be an author. My name will be on the book—Maria Sandoval!"

Mom looked expectantly again at her parents' faces. She had longed for twenty years to see them looking proud of her. They loved her, and they loved their grandchildren. She always knew that. But they had always been disappointed in her, especially *Abuela* Eva. She knew that too.

Mom's parents rose and came to her to embrace her.

Ernesto felt a rush of heartfelt happiness. He knew how much Mom wanted to make her parents proud, just as *he* was eager to make his parents proud. He knew how proud his Sandoval grandparents were when their son graduated *magna cum laude* from the university.

Now, at last, Maria Sandoval saw the look in her parents eyes that she had yearned for for so long.

Mrs. Sandoval's cousins peppered her with enthusiastic questions. Her parents sat very quietly, *Abuelo* Al grinning at his daughter. *Abuela* Eva, for once, had little to say. For a long while, they all chattered about the news and about other things.

As they did, Ernesto realized that a light had been shined on an old family secret. Actually, it was not a secret. Everyone knew about it, but no one talked about it. It was a secret only in that sense.

The light, Ernesto thought, had been shined on other, darker secrets. Fernando Sanchez and Rosalie Rivas no longer shared a dreadful secret. The road ahead for them would be difficult. But taking it was easier than the path they'd been on.

Bullying and abuse were losing their grip on the Martinez household. And that was partly because Naomi had decided take a stand with her father. She had decided to be her own person—and maybe someday to be his girl.